DYLAN MCFINN & THE SEA SERPENT'S FURY

LIAM S JENKINS

FOREWORD

Dreamer, air head, away with the fairies, weirdo. These are all terms and phrases I'm sure you've heard from time to time if you have an imagination like mine.

If you haven't, and all you want is to read a good story, then you've come to the right place.

But, if you're like me and you love drawing, writing, making up fantastic new worlds, characters and their friends then please hear my call – because you're needed now more than ever.

Many thousands of years ago, creatives were considered the most important people in their communities. Stories, songs, poems and paintings were all considered sacred tools and moral compasses from which people learned and received guidance. But the importance of creativity has been forgotten along with storytelling and its important role within a community.

I believe that as a civilisation we are at the tipping point of losing our way, losing our stories and guidance; stories of heroes, heroines and all things magical.

I wrote this book with no real experience, but with the hope that it would be read by, inflame, and perhaps inspire maybe just one creative of the next generation to follow the path less trodden. If, as a civilisation, we continue down this road of superficial and self-centred values ... then we're really going to need your help.

I hope you enjoy the book, and I hope you find room for imagination in your life.

Liam Jenkins
  January 2019

JOIN THE DYLAN MCFINN UNIVERSE

Before you begin the plunge into the Dylan McFinn Universe, consider joining the Dylan McFinn members' club to get free e-books and unique items that will accompany the book and give you a deeper insight into the history of Maloto.

Members are always first to hear about news and new books and publications.

See the back of the book for details on how to sign up.

PRELUDE

Where our journey begins ...

The Fijian night sky was illuminated by millions of stars. Palm trees gently swayed in the Pacific wind. In the distance, you could hear waves softly breaking on the shore. The evening marked a great occasion on the small island of Maloto, when all the villagers came together once a year to celebrate its history.

The air was filled with joy and laughter as hundreds of villagers gathered on the beach. Trees and huts were decorated with brightly coloured lanterns. Flaming bamboo torches lit the way to the gathering. Adults supped the famous Maloto Cannonball rum from painted coconuts.

A spritely young woman played a flute accompanied by passers-by, clapping and cheering to her jubilant tune of *Spanish Ladies*.

From the old lighthouse a small group started to emerge; they seemed to be waiting for somebody. Lots of excited children swarmed around a hunched, wizened old man as he also appeared from the old lighthouse and started to make his way gingerly through the gate and down to the beach, leaning on a walking stick every so often for a rest.

Dozens of little boys and girls joined his journey, jumping and hopping with anticipation of what was to come. Holding an old nose warmer pipe, he patted the closest one on the head affectionately before speaking to the crowd of children.

"Now, now, little ones, settle down, settle down, let me get to my seat. If you don't settle down, then how can I begin the story?" he said as he made his way onto the beach. The beautiful white sand looked like a brilliant white carpet, sparkling in the lantern light.

As he sat down in the chair they had placed for him near the open beach fire, he was met with a chorus of cheers and applause. Gradually, the crowd began to quieten down and sat around the old man, ready for him to begin.

Not only children, but adults of all ages also started to join the group. The old man shuffled forward in his seat, which was decorated in vibrant colours and palm leaves. He pulled a battered old satchel closer to him, reached in and took out an equally old-looking leather-bound book. The front of the book was embossed with faded gold lettering. It read *The Tales of Brother McFinn*.

The old man had soft, wavy, silver hair and his face was craggy and weather-beaten. One deep distinctive scar was carved on his left cheek, from his ear to the base of his nose.

A hush of anticipation fell over the crowd as he opened up the book to the first page.

He took a puff on his pipe, looked up at all the adoring faces and his eyes began to fill with tears of pride. A lump rose in his throat and he took a moment to compose himself.

In a croaky voice, he addressed the crowd. "Welcome, Malotans and mini Malotans!" Cheering and applause rumbled across the gathered crowd. His gaze grew distant and he stared into the flames, staring into the past and what could have been.

He slowly came to and continued his introduction. "For those who don't know me, my name is Dylan McFinn and you all know me as the steward of the lighthouse, but I'm about to tell you who I really am! We're here on this wonderful, momentous evening to celebrate, and to share an equally wonderful and momentous story. It's a story about friends, family, monsters, myths, magic, love, sacrifice and triumph."

He looked down at the children, took a further draw on his nose warmer pipe and exhaled into the air, creating a cloud of very sweet-smelling smoke. His face broke through the haze and he spoke to them directly. "Little ones. If you are to remember one thing from this story, I want it to be this.

"I want you all to remember that no matter how small you think you are, you can all change the world with one single thought or action. All you have to do is believe that you can. Therein lies the magic.

"The world we live in is a truly wonderful place, filled with magic and mystery. Never forget that magic is all around you, magic is love and kindness, when all is lost love will pull you through the darkest of times."

Dylan sat back, took a deep breath and started reading. "As in all the best journeys, it all starts with an unsuspecting hero, unaware that his life is about to change forever ..."

CHAPTER 1
STRANGE GOINGS ON IN BOTTLE NECK BAY

Drip ... drip ... drip ... drip ... The drumbeat of droplets hitting water from a distance began to stir the slumped frame of the Sea Captain as he sat in a weathered armchair at Neptune's Tower, a favourite tavern for well-seasoned sailors.

Mmpphh ... he lifted his head up and squinted painfully to investigate where the noise was coming from.

His eyes eventually fixed on a battered old slop bucket, spilling over with suspiciously coloured water. The dripping was coming from a revolting-looking rag above it. The drops of murky water continued to fall into the beaten bucket.

A rancid smell slowly wafted over, clinging to his nose hairs and suddenly hitting the back of his throat like a sledgehammer.

The Captain lifted his head up and closed his eyes, trying to mask the smell by pinching his nose and breathing through his mouth.

He then heard a noise he couldn't identify. It went, "Naruokeh?" It sounded familiar, but he couldn't quite work out what it was.

He heard it again, in front of him. Still unable to understand the sound, he opened his eyes slowly and started to focus on the large pink blurry blob in front of him.

He picked a lodged peanut out from the corner of his mouth as he had one last try to figure out what the blob was.

"Are you OK?"

Ahh ... now ... this he recognised. His memory shunted sharply back into place as he remembered where he was, and what he'd been doing before he passed out in an extremely comfortable armchair.

After his daily shift in the lighthouse, the Captain would always visit his lifelong friend Rusty Irwin. Rusty was an extremely tall, thick-set mountain of a man with a great interest in mixing plants and potions – mainly for recreational use. Rusty took great pleasure in perfecting his infamous Cannonball rum and testing out its potency on his regular visitors.

Rusty. It was Rusty. This time with a tone of impatience in his voice, he said, "Captain ... Are you OK? Yes or no?"

"Nope – hic – I'm not being your guinea pig again! Enough is enough," he slurred. "My stomach feels like a sloop on a stormy sea."

Rusty scoffed. "So a bit delicate then? Can't be anything to do with the new Cannonball rum. It's a really weak batch."

"Perhaps it was those mackerel heads I had for dinner earlier," said the Captain.

"You've made a bit of a mess, Culbert, old friend – and Eric doesn't value your custom as much as I do." Rusty gestured over his left shoulder with his thumb toward Eric, a scrawny, dark-haired young man who was Rusty's help at Neptune's Tower. Holding a bucket full of something stinking and unpleasant, he shot the Captain a disapproving look. "That's the last time I clean up your mess."

"Sorry, Eric. You know I can never turn down a challenge

– hic – but I appreciate you cleaning up after me. I'm very sorry for the mess. You must be compensated." He fumbled in his pocket, separating the fluff and dried seaweed from his loose change. His fingers rubbed across a coin and flicked it in the direction of the slim-framed boy.

In Eric's haste, he went to catch the coin with both hands, forgetting he was holding the overflowing bucket. He caught the coin just as the full bucket hit the orange terracotta tiles with a loud 'KA-DOINK!'

The contents of the bucket exploded across Eric's recently cleaned floor. "Oh, for the love of Neptune's beard!" Eric bellowed, squeezing the coin until the tips of his fingers turned white.

"You're cleaning that up again, you clumsy dolt!" boomed Rusty.

Cursing, Eric picked up the bucket and went to get the mop for the second time that evening.

The Captain reached into his pocket again and looked across at Rusty. "So how much do I owe you?"

Running through quick calculations on his thick fingers, Rusty replied, "Call it forty-five?"

"Pleasure doing business with you." The Captain slapped a handful of crumpled notes and dirty coins on the table and attempted to get out of the very comfy leather chair. He looked out of the window, startled.

"It's dark?" he said.

"Well – it is nearly midnight," said Rusty. "You've been slumped in that chair for four and a half hours now, and the only reason I haven't given you the old heave-ho is that we're friends."

"Better head home, then! Don't want to outstay my welcome." The Captain placed both feet on the floor, avoiding the sprawling river of brown slurry, and meandered gingerly toward the door.

The interesting thing about Neptune's Tower was that it had no actual location, but appeared in various spots on Maloto Island.

The tower itself was covered in shimmering golden tiles and shot several hundred feet into the sky, almost touching the clouds. In legend, the tower was supposed to have magical powers. Although used by many a salty sea dog from far and wide of the Pacific Ocean, nobody really knew its history, or why it appeared at sundown every night ... and disappeared every midnight.

Rusty and Eric lived on the ground floor of the tower. The rest was out of bounds and not accessible to landlubbers.

Many had tried to secure the location of the tower, but all seafaring folk had failed – apart from the Captain.

So, not wanting to vanish in a puff of smoke with the tower, the Captain shut the heavy studded wooden door behind him and wandered out onto the soft white moonlit sand, the warm, gentle sea air instantly calming his unsettled stomach. The stars danced on the rippling water. The soft and soothing wind felt alive and seemed to swirl around him, helping him along the shore.

Suddenly he heard a fizzing sound behind him – FFFFFTTTTT! – and there was a flash of white light. He turned around. The tower had disappeared into thin air.

"Must be midnight," said the Captain to himself, and carried on his wayward trip home.

The Captain – a grizzly-looking man with a wild, untamed bushy beard – worked as the lighthouse keeper in Bottle Neck Bay, giving safety to all ships passing through the island's waters. His arms were covered in nautical tattoos, each telling its own tale of the seven seas.

The Captain was one of the most courageous and fearless captains of his time, and he was known to all sailors and seafarers across the seven seas. He had made many friends over the years. But apart from a small green parrot called Adrian, he lived alone in Bottle Neck Bay.

When he wasn't working the lighthouse or propping up the bar at Neptune's Tower, he tirelessly helped the locals by keeping the island clean and free of pollution with his ideas and inventions for recycling.

The Captain began to sing merrily in the darkness while gazing across the tepid waters of the bay. "Farewell and adieu to you, Spanish ladies, Farewell and adieu to you ladies of Sp —" He stopped in his tracks, his feet sinking in the warm, wet sand as he saw an unfamiliar shape in the water. Something that he'd never seen before.

Putting it down to the Cannonball rum, he continued his song. "... for we have received orders for sail to old Engl—" There it was again. The water was swelling unnaturally. He caught a glimpse of something shimmering; emerald greens and sapphire blues flashed through the waters ... He wasn't sure what it was, but it seemed to be calling to him.

He began to walk into the gentle break of the waves on the beach, thinking that it might be an emperor angelfish in distress. He knew that they often found themselves in shallow water and needed to be pushed back into deeper currents.

He wandered out further. He was up to his waist now, and the object seemed to be coming straight toward him. He held his ground and dug his feet into the wet sand, ready to grapple with ... whatever it was.

The object was heading directly for him, faster and faster, pushing a rising wave before it. Bracing for impact, the Captain put one foot behind the other ... then a large fin appeared from the darkness and splashed him straight in the face, blinding him for a moment. It seemed deliberate.

The large fish then flew up into the midnight air. As it arched over his head, he still couldn't see what it was. Its tail hit him in the chest, making him fall on his bottom and leaving only his head now poking out of the water.

The fish landed with a splash, and the aftermath hit the Captain in the face again.

Flailing, coughing and spluttering, he quickly readied himself to wrestle with the monster. He rubbed his eyes to try and clear his vision and he caught a glimpse, but it couldn't be ... he shook his head and looked again. Surely not?

This was no emperor angelfish, but a mermaid! He couldn't believe his eyes and clambered to his feet, trying to think of what to say.

"Are you real?" he called into the darkness.

"Well, hello to you, too!" said a soft voice. "My name is Varuna, and yes, I am. A real mermaid. What about you? Are you real?"

Steadying himself, the Captain looked again, trying to clear the salt water from his stinging eyes. There she was, the legendary mythical creature. A mermaid.

Many sailors spoke of the beauty of mermaids, of their white porcelain skin and flowing red hair. But most believed them to be the stuff of legend. How could a creature with the body of a woman and the tail of a fish be real? Explorers, pirates, admirals and merchant sailors alike could spend their whole lives on the ocean waves without seeing a glimpse of a mermaid.

"But mermaids aren't real, you're not real, you can't be, you're just a myth!" the Captain said. "Or a side effect of that rum."

"Oh, really?" replied Varuna, flicking her tail to soak the Captain for a third time, and knocking him over again. "What was that, then? Can a myth do that?"

"I ... I guess not," said the flummoxed Captain. He had seaweed on the top of his head, giving the impression that he had a head of scraggly knotted green hair.

A mermaid's beauty can leave a mere mortal spellbound, completely mesmerised – especially if seen under the evening sky at twilight. Varuna's beauty was immeasurable.

Her tail shimmered with flecks of purple, green and turquoise as she swam around Culbert, laughing playfully as she did so. "Sing me more of that song," she said.

"What song?" he replied, swiping the seaweed from the top of his head and clambering to stand up.

"The song you were singing on the beach."

Completely perplexed, he tried to retrace the thoughts he'd had before he ended up in the water. "Oh right, yes, I remember: the Spanish ladies."

"Yes, that one – I liked it," said Varuna, continuing to circle the Captain.

"OK." He slapped his chest pocket and an arc of salty water shot up into the air. With water running off his sleeves like a water slide, he began to sing. "Farewell and adieu to you, Spanish ladies, Farewell and adieu to you, ladies of Spain ..."

Varuna stopped circling and slowly swam closer to listen. Her smile widened as he continued to serenade her in the warm waters.

He continued, "... for we have received orders for sail to old England ..."

Varuna was now within touching distance. She reached for the Captain's hand. He held it out and their hands touched for the first time.

"See, I told you I was real!"

Utterly captivated by this creature, the Captain began to stutter and stammer and lost his place in the song.

"What's your name?" said Varuna softly.

"My Friends call me Captain ... but my real name is Culbert McFinn."

"Well, Culbert McFinn, that was a lovely song. Thank you for singing it for me."

Still holding his hand, Varuna used the Captain's arm as a lever to pull herself up out of the water – and in one sweeping movement she stole a kiss from his cheek and flipped herself over his head, knocking him back into the water.

Laughing loudly, she began to swim away.

"See you around, Culbert McFinn!"

With that she disappeared into the dark waters. Quickly getting to his feet, he tried to see if she was still in sight, but she had vanished into the midnight blue.

"Where are you going? Will I ever see you again?" Culbert shouted into the darkness ... but there was no response. He turned left and right, trying to see if she had swum behind him.

"Varuna?!"

Nothing.

Crestfallen, and questioning whether this was a hallucination brought on by the unproofed Cannonball rum, the Captain began to wade back to the shore.

With every few steps he kept turning around, looking to see if she had returned, but there was no sign of her. With his head bowed, he continued the long walk back to Bottle Neck Bay where a warm fire and his comfortable hammock awaited him at the lighthouse.

CHAPTER 2
STARTING WITH A PARROT
CALLED ADRIAN

The sun was bleeding through the thin hessian curtains. Contorted in his hammock, the Captain resembled the shape of a king prawn.

The crisscross pattern of the hammock had left marks on his face, and his beard had gone all curly due to the salt water from his midnight escapade with Varuna the night before.

The sun was warm and comforting on his face, but not bright enough to wake him up fully. His eyes closed and he began to think of Varuna again; he tried to picture her face but sadly the image was fading.

Doof, doof, doof, doof, doof ...

He opened an eye.

"Adrian, is that you?"

"Brawk! Man the barricades, load the cannons! Brawk!" screeched Adrian.

"No, it's not him," thought the Captain.

Louder this time – DOOF, DOOF, DOOF.

"What was that?" he said softly, pushing his dixie cup hat out of his eye line as he glanced hazily at the clock. Nine forty-five ...

"Neptune's beard! I'm late!"

He went to get out of his hammock, but in his haste to get up he rocked from side to side, and the hammock flipped him out. He fell flat on his face, knocking over a number of copper pots and pans on the floor with a mighty clatter.

"Brawk! Sack the juggler, brawk, enjoy the trip?!" squawked Adrian, filled with glee at the Captain's misfortune.

"Shush, you poor excuse for a feather duster – carry on like that and I'll take you to the taxidermist, you stupid bird!"

Scrambling to his feet, he got his foot jammed in a copper kettle. He flapped around like a fish out of water, banging and crashing into his kitchen and then into the front room, looking for his keys.

"Where are they?" he said, scratching his head and quickly scanning the room, before spotting the keys hiding on his armchair, where he had left them the night before.

He launched himself at the chair.

"Oh, bloody hell!"

The set of keys, now having a mind of their own, seemed to be jumping around the chair restlessly, like a little sprat trying to avoid capture by a pursuing conger eel.

"Captain, Captain! Is that you?" said a muffled voice from outside the lighthouse door.

"Be right with you!" said the Captain, all in a fluster.

He grabbed the keys with both hands and rolled over the chair. As his copper-kettle-clad foot hit the tiled floor, it made a clonking sound that filled the room.

"Brawk – take cover, man the cannons, we're under attack! Brawk!" bellowed Adrian.

Culbert growled at him to shut up. Getting to his feet, he ran to the door with intermittent clunks from his trapped foot. He skidded a couple of feet from the door before slamming into it with a loud crash.

Culbert heard a yelp of alarm from the unknown visitor on the other side of the door.

The Captain scratched desperately at the door, trying to find the keyhole. At last, he heard the click of the lock and opened the door with an urgent whoosh.

"Are you alright?" said the anonymous figure.

Culbert recognised him instantly. "Good morning, Marvin," he said, trying to compose himself and pretending not to remember that he was late for their morning engagement. "What can I do for you?"

Marvin stared down at the foot wedged in the copper pot with a curious look on his face.

Culbert caught his gaze.

"What? This thing? Yes ... it's a new invention I'm trying out ... top secret. Sends tiger sharks mad! I'm working on it for one of the villagers. Can't tell you who, though," he said, tapping the side of his nose. "So ... what can I do for you?" He continued to pretend that he didn't know why Marvin was there.

Marvin – a short, stout fellow stinking of a pungent mixture of crab and seaweed – extended his hand to shake Culbert's. For years he had been fighting a battle against the enormous amount of plastic that washed up in the waters around Maloto.

"My good man, you said that you would help me fix my plastic-catching nets this morning, and modify them so that we can catch more plastic. Had you forgotten?"

"Oh, Blackbeard's ghost! Yes, I did, didn't I? Give me a minute and I'll be right with you."

He turned and scooted off into the lighthouse, shutting the door abruptly behind him. There shortly followed lots of muffled grunts and groans as he tried to get the kettle off his foot.

Marvin turned away and began to walk around the small

garden outside the front of the lighthouse to pass the time. Ducking under the washing line full of sardines and mackerel drying out in the morning sun, Marvin began to talk to the Captain through the open kitchen window.

"Did you see anything strange last night down by the coast, Capt? There's been reports of a mysterious green and blue glow out by Peanut Cove. Some even said it looked like the shape of a woman."

Marvin turned around and inspected the abundant herb garden, under the kitchen window. He bent down to smell a heaving bush of fragrant lavender and continued to talk to the outside of the lighthouse.

"Yes, very strange behaviour – you don't think it could be a ...?"

The door swung open abruptly. Culbert was completely changed and no longer had a copper kettle stuck on his foot.

He replied sharply, "They don't exist, Marvin. It was probably just *Noctiluca scintillans*."

Marvin stopped smelling the lavender and stood up. He looked directly at Culbert with a puzzled expression. "What's *Noctiluca scintillans*?"

"Plankton. Little sea-glowing blighters that get together in big clumps and make the water glow green or blue. That's probably what the glow was."

Although he knew full well that the closest spotted school of phytoplankton was over ten thousand kilometres away in the Far East, Culbert made sure to keep this under his hat, hoping to play down his sighting of Varuna last night.

"Shall we get going then? Those nets won't modify themselves!"

"I guess so."

In one flowing movement, Culbert reached up to the clothes line, whipped off one of the dried mackerel and chucked it back through the open kitchen window, He waited and then he heard a satisfying thwack, then a squawk, then a thud. "Got the little sod!"

He put his hand at the base of Marvin's back to guide him hastily out of the garden and into the town, hoping his answer would baffle him enough to stop any further questions.

"So, Marvin my friend, tell me more about these nets," said the Captain.

The pair walked alongside each other through the colourful, vibrant market of Maloto, which was brimming with people from the village, all buying their groceries and other everyday essentials.

Maloto prided itself on recycling items found in the sea and on the shore. All items for sale in the market had been recycled or repurposed.

Everyone knew the Captain, because he had helped most of them retrieve rubbish from the sea. The stallholders all waved and gestured to him as he walked by their stall.

Marvin, undeterred by the Captain's attempts to blindside him by throwing fish and changing the subject, continued his questioning.

"I don't think it was phytoplankton, Capt. I think it was a mermaid. Many islanders think so, too."

Unimpressed by Marvin's tenacity, Culbert thought he would try a different tack. He stopped by the nearest stall and started rummaging through it for a nicknack that he needed to help him fix the nets.

"Marvin ... I spent over twenty-five years sailing the seven seas; I've seen things that you wouldn't believe. I've seen barnacles the size of footballs, narwhals the size of boats, and giant squid so big they could pull an ocean liner to the murky depths with their monstrous tentacles – but there are no such things as mermaids."

"But ..."

The Captain continued to make his point without even looking up from the table of hidden treasures, bits of plastic, spinning lures and hooks.

"Even Christopher Columbus thought he had seen three mermaids off the coast of the Dominican Republic. But when he got closer to reality, they turned out to be manatees, not mermaids. Marvin, mermaids don't exist. If they did – I would have seen one!"

"Perhaps you're right – probably just a manatee, they are known to circle the harbour from time to time." Marvin still looked dubious.

"Precisely," said the Captain sharply. "Can we just leave all this silly talk of mermaids now?" He hoped that Marvin had been thrown off the scent completely.

Marvin huffed and dropped his questioning.

Culbert handed the stall owner a handful of golden pandanas and pointed at a strange item on the table. The stall owner nodded, and Culbert picked up the object and put it in his pocket.

Changing the subject, he began to talk about the modification of Marvin's nets. "So, going back to my original question, tell me about your nets. What's wrong with them?"

Marvin pulled up his belt to his belly button and began to explain his process to the Captain.

"Well, normally I go to the usual spot – where the rubbish gets caught up in the current – put in the nets and whip out as much rubbish as we can, no danger, no fuss."

He sighed. "But of late, the currents are mysteriously getting stronger and our nets aren't working. They keep breaking and we haven't been able to hold anything, not a sausage!"

Culbert stroked his bushy beard in silence as the two men walked onwards down the cobbled streets to Dolphin Harbour, where Marvin's boat was anchored.

CHAPTER 3

FLYING FOX

"Here we are."

Marvin pointed in the direction of his boat, the infamous Flying Fox, a stinking, rusty old decommissioned fishing boat. In its time it had been one of the flagships of the Malotan fishing fleet; although it was small, it was nimble, fast and virtually unsinkable. The old warhorse was bobbing gently in the harbour, with all of Marvin's nets piled neatly on the harbour wall alongside.

The Captain wandered over to the Flying Fox and tapped its side affectionately. "Ah, old friend, they don't make them like you any more. We had some great adventures ..."

Marvin smiled. "I couldn't let them send her to the breaker's yard after all we'd gone through together – she's part of the family!"

"Quite right!" agreed the Captain. "This little warrior has saved me from many a tight spot. It's good to see the old girl, glad she's in the hands of someone who knows a little about boats!"

The Captain continued to reminisce for a few moments

and then began to inspect the nets. "Yes ... hmm ... I see," he murmured as he ran the rough rope through his hands. "Yep, we can fix this. We'll have these in the water and catching masses of plastic in no time!"

Marvin was invading Culbert's space, bending over and inspecting what he was doing very closely. Culbert turned to him. "I'm parched. You couldn't run and get this old sea dog a glass of water from the Dolphin, could you?"

The Dolphin was the old tavern at the top of the harbour; it was very popular with all of the fisherman and sailors. Always good for a whale of a tale and a black eye.

As soon as Marvin bumbled off the boat and in the direction of the tavern, the Captain went to work. Like all good sailors, he knew that legends of the high seas come with their own precious secrets – including any modifications they may make to their vessels.

Marvin had been too busy questioning the Captain about mermaids on their walk through the market and hadn't noticed what he had bought: an old windsock that had long since been declared useless at an airport, and some wooden curtain hooks.

Culbert promptly pulled the windsock out of his pocket and unravelled it. He tied one end off with fishing line and wafted it above his head, making sure to catch as much air as he could, and pinched it off. He then tied off the other end. It looked like a huge orange sausage.

He pushed his weight against it, and it gave a decent amount of resistance without deflating.

"Perfect! Now for the hooks," he muttered.

The luminous orange sausage had a thin rope running around the outside of it. Culbert grabbed a handful of curtain hooks and began fixing them to the rope.

His theory was that when the net was placed in the water

it would act like a massive curtain, catching all the rubbish right down to the sea bed, while the fish could swim right through the holes in the net.

Now all he had to do was to affix the nets to the curtain hooks and voila! An instant, floating, orange plastic-catching curtain!

Marvin wandered back over and handed him a glass of water. "Marvellous!" replied the Captain, snatching it from Marvin and quaffing the whole glass in one. "Ahh ... all finished, shall we go and try them out?"

Marvin looked astonished. "You've finished them already?" he said dubiously.

"Lovely glass of water, that! Adam's ale, you know! Yep, all done – shall we go? Come on, you can help me put them onboard the Flying Fox."

Still perplexed, Marvin looked at the Captain in disbelief, then inspected his nets. He noticed the curtain hooks – and the windsock.

"What's this?" He pointed at the big orange sausage and lifted it up by one end.

"That, my friend, is what will make you the most famous plastic catcher this side of the Pacific."

Still looking puzzled, Marvin questioned him further. "A windsock? Why? It's not like I need to know where the wind is blowing when we're on the ocean. How's it going to work?"

The Captain sighed. "Come along, Marvin – I much prefer the practical. Just help me load them onto the boat and I can show you! All these questions are getting quite tedious."

Marvin nodded and stopped his barrage of questions. He picked up the other end of the windsock, along with the nets, and started to load them on to the Flying Fox with Culbert.

Once the pair had loaded all the nets onto the boat,

making sure that they didn't get them caught or tangled together, Marvin moved into the cockpit and turned on the engines. He took in the lines and weighed anchor. Culbert stood proudly at the bow with his hands behind his back, enjoying the glorious morning sun on his face.

They bobbed out of the harbour and into open sea. Marvin opened up the engines and the little Flying Fox began to roar, churning out plumes of diesel smoke in its wake. The salty sea air gently blew over Culbert's craggy beard. He took in a deep breath ...

"Ahh, that smell – you really can't beat it, the smell of adventure," he said, then turned around to Marvin. "Ain't that right, First Mate?"

"WHAT?" said Marvin, cupping his hand to his ear, trying to hear Culbert through the thick pane of glass in the cockpit and over the chugging engine.

"I said, YOU CAN'T BEAT THE SMELL!"

"WHAT ... DIESEL??" said Marvin with a look of bemusement, not for the first time that morning.

"Oh, just forget it," said the Captain, exasperated.

"WHAT!?!?" shouted Marvin.

"NEVER MIND!!!"

"WHAT?????"

"For the love of Poseidon ..." Culbert waved at Marvin as he knew this conversation was short-lived.

The bow rose and dipped through the Fijian waves; every now and again a wave would break and an explosion of sea water and spray filled the air.

Culbert turned to look along Maloto's spectacular coast-line. They had just passed Bottle Neck Bay and his light-house, heading north out into the Pacific.

The cliff side rose steadily, showing off the wonderful layered colours of its sedimentary rock. Nestled on top were lush, dark green palm trees and vegetation; below, the brilliant white sand running unspoilt for miles and miles. It was a beautiful sight to behold, and he was filled with a huge sense of pride and love for his island.

The wind blew again across the Captain's face, only this time it seemed to be saying something.

"Culbert! Culbert McFinn – I can see you!"

Pride quickly turned to confusion and he shook his head. He must be hearing things. He shook his head but again the wind softly whispered, "Culbert ... sing me that song again ..."

Thinking it was his pot-bellied friend playing a trick on him, he turned around quickly to look at Marvin. Marvin was concentrating at the helm with his tongue sticking out, staying true to his course. There was no sign of amusement on his face.

Marvin waved at him, then put his hand up to cup his mouth. "Won't be long now – another half an hour, I reckon!" he shouted.

The Captain put up his thumb to avoid another pointless conversation.

It wasn't Marvin, that was for sure.

Putting it down to a rough night but still a little disconcerted, he took up his place again at the bow.

He watched as the waters changed from a translucent light blue to a deeper, more sinister, teal – a true sign that they were getting into deeper waters and closer to the tip of the reef – the Purple Wall.

His head was still pounding from the Cannonball rum he'd drunk the night before; that glass of water had only temporarily taken the edge off his headache.

Looking for a place to catch a quick snooze, he stepped down from the bow and made an impromptu bed out of the rope the anchor was tied to.

He tilted his hat forward over his eyes and let the rocking of the boat send him to sleep.

There she was again, so vividly beautiful in his dreams, he wanted to stay there forever. The brief meeting with Varuna played over and over again in his mind. Each time it ended, it faded to black and restarted again in an instant like an old film on loop.

CHAPTER 4
AT HOME ON THE OCEAN

S tirring from his brief slumber, Culbert tipped his hat up off his brow and blinked directly up into the sky. The clouds gently drifting past the sun offered only fleeting shade. He rubbed at his itching cheek where it had rested on the rope pillow.

There was no other place he would rather be than on the sea. It always felt like home, even at its most tempestuous and violent. This was where he belonged.

His serenity was shattered abruptly.

"WE'RE HERE!!" shouted Marvin.

He sat up and turned to look at the ocean. True enough, just as Marvin had promised, the Flying Fox was surrounded by thousands of bottles, bags, and other plastic nick-nackery, all floating and bobbing around them like a fluther of fantastical jellyfish.

Culbert sighed and shook his head. The floating debris stretched as far as the eye could see. "When will people learn?" he muttered to himself.

"DROP ANCHOR, THIS IS THE SPOT!!" bellowed Marvin.

"Aye aye," said the Captain, and quick as a flash he hopped off the makeshift rope bed, grabbed hold of the anchor and tossed it overboard with an almighty splash.

He whirred into life and turned his attention to the nets. The windsock was already inflated, ready to be the star of the show, but the real test was to see if it would float.

Marvin turned off the engines and everything went quiet. There was only the gentle swell of the waves breaking and lapping on the side of the Flying Fox.

Culbert picked up the windsock and threw it overboard. Success! It floated!

Reeling it back in, he pulled it back onboard and then attached the nets to the curtain hooks before throwing the whole assembly back into the ocean.

He watched as each net section tumbled off the side of the boat in sequence.

He took out his nose warmer from his pocket. His most favoured of possessions, given to him by his grandfather, it was a stubby little pipe. He drew on it hard, screwing up his eyes, trying to light the damp tobacco.

The last net flew off into the salty waters below just as he finally lit his pipe. He held it in his left hand, smouldering away, while his right held the rope that was attached to the floating windsock.

"That's it, Marvin, they're all in the water!" said Culbert.

Marvin's face lit up with glee and he slapped Culbert on the shoulder as they watched the currents dragging the plastic bounty to his modified contraption. Now all they had to do was wait and hope it worked.

He came to join Culbert and sat at the bow of the boat as they watched all the precious plastic gathering around the side of the windsock.

"So, has it worked?" Marvin said hopefully, looking over

the side of the boat to where the windsock was bobbing triumphantly in the sapphire-blue waters.

"Patience, my rotund little friend." He slapped Marvin on the back. "This will work, just give it some time – let the majestic Pacific current work its magic."

The two waited patiently as the deep blue Pacific continued to bounce the boat around like a cork in a bottle while the scorching sun beat down on their heads. Culbert began to wish he had a bigger hat.

He dipped his fingers over the side and cupped a handful of sea water. He sprinkled some into his pipe and started to draw on it once more. Marvin looked at him, confused.

Before he could ask, the Captain said, "Keeps the tobacco moist. Also gives it a nice salty twist."

And with that, he struck a match on the side of the boat, relit his nose warmer, took a puff and turned to look out to sea.

A plume of malodorous smoke wafted over to Marvin. He waved the air to clear it, then started to cough and splutter. Oblivious to his friend's discomfort, Culbert smiled as his mind wandered to Varuna once more, trying to reimagine her beauty.

He closed his eyes and let the sun's warm rays caress his face – but then a shiver went down his spine. He opened his eyes but couldn't shake the thought that something large was nearby. Varuna? She felt nearby, she felt present.

Marvin was looking straight out to sea, watching the shimmering of the waves and completely unaware of the unnerving look on Culbert's face. He picked at the dried paint on the side of the boat and pushed the freed flecks overboard.

He focused on the bobbing windsock once more, then stood up impatiently. "Right, Capt, so when are we going to bring these nets in? They've been out there a good hour or so, they must have tonnes of plastic in there by now!"

"Not yet," replied the Captain, staring out to sea.

Ignoring him completely, Marvin asked, "Shall I start bringing them in, then?"

Culbert sighed. Knowing that this was a battle of wits that he'd already lost, he gestured with his hand. "Start bringing the nets in then, you guppy!"

Marvin frowned at Culbert and leaned over the boat. He reached into the water, grabbing the wet rope and beginning to haul in the windsock and the nets.

The windsock bounced up against the side of the boat and after a minute or so of strenuous pulling on the heavy rope, he dragged it onboard; behind it, the nets began to come to the surface.

"Neptune's trident!" shouted Marvin with glee as the first net flopped onto the deck. "There must be over ten pounds of plastic there!"

His pace quickened; he was desperate to see the next net. He lifted it over the boat's side and closely examined the plastic bounty. "Culbert McFinn, you bloomin' genius!"

Elated, he grabbed the rope again and started to pull with all his might, frantic with anticipation for the next net and its plastic cargo.

The net came into view. "There's even more in this one!"

The Captain extinguished his pipe, knocked it against the side of the boat and put it in his pocket. He walked across to help his jubilant friend.

Each net that surfaced brought with it an enormous quantity of plastic. Marvin jigged around and punched the air.

"See, I told you it would make you the most famous plastic merchant in the Pacific! Just think – you can sell all this to the islanders for recycling," said Culbert.

The pair were down to the last net. The Captain gestured

to Marvin. "I'll bring the last one in, friend, you go and check out your bounty."

Culbert walked over to the rope and took it out of Marvin's hand. He tugged hard, but the net seemed to be stuck on something.

"Hmm, must be stuck on a bit of reef." He pulled harder ... nothing ... harder still ... nothing but resistance. It wasn't budging. He took off his hat and scratched his head. "It makes no sense: we're not over any reef, the depth here is well over forty metres, so why is it stuck?"

Too elated with his gigantic plastic stash, Marvin shrugged. "Just keep pulling, if you can't shift it we'll just cut it free," he said, then carried on separating plastic.

This was clearly a task Culbert was going to have to sort on his own. He looked over the side of the boat to get a better view. He reached into the water to try and free the net from whatever it was caught on.

Before he even had time to blink, a hand appeared from the dark blue waters and grabbed his shirt, pulling him in.

Shocked, the Captain let out an almighty scream, then very quickly hit the waves with a loud splash. Marvin turned around to see what had happened.

Momentarily frozen by the coldness of the water but recovering quickly, Culbert was now furiously thrashing around, desperate to see who or what had pulled him in.

It was Varuna! She must have been following the boat. She corkscrewed around the Captain until she was face to face with him ... although his eyes were blurry and burning from the salt and he couldn't entirely trust them, he knew it was her.

With one powerful flick of her tail, she turned downwards and proceeded to dive, grabbing the Captain's ankle as she did so.

Panicking, his mind racing, he began to swim furiously

upwards as he thought she was going to drown him. Although he was a champion swimmer who could hold his breath underwater for over four minutes, this alarmed him.

"Captain? Captain? Where are you? What happened?" shouted Marvin hopelessly at the water. "Culbert? Did you free that last net? How much plastic was in it?"

The Captain started to feel the pressure and temperature change of the water as Varuna dragged him ever deeper. Trying to free his leg, he started to kick as hard as he could, hoping the mermaid's grip would loosen.

Eventually she did let go, knowing how much distress Culbert was enduring. He immediately began to swim toward the surface, which felt like an eternity away.

Varuna chased him. When she caught up, she wrapped herself around him ... and then she did something even more unexpected, as the blue water refracted the sunlight around them. With gentle, loving lips, she kissed him.

CHAPTER 5
SAVED BY A BUBBLE

"Culbert! This isn't funny any more!" Marvin screamed at the water. He rushed to the helm of the boat and scrambled for his binoculars to see if the Captain had been carried away in a strong underwater current.

Manic, he squinted out to sea, searching for a head bobbing up and down or somebody waving for help.

"Captain, for Neptune's sake! Black tips and tigers hunt and feed in this channel! Come on, buddy, where are you?" said Marvin to himself.

Meanwhile, under the water, Culbert opened his eyes, still reeling from the tender kiss. In his astonishment he could see Varuna clear as crystal, but he was rapidly running out of breath. He was beginning to feel light-headed. He took a last look at her, then raised his head to the ocean surface. He shook his head and began to swim upwards.

As his feet pushed past her, Varuna grabbed his ankle once again and pulled him back down. She then opened her hand and blew bubbles across it. Still terrified of drowning and not quite understanding what was happening around him, he made his third attempt to swim for the surface.

However, the bubbles she blew were growing in size, larger and larger ... until one was as big as him. This giant bubble started to surround him.

As soon as the bubble had covered him and completed the seal, he could breathe. He took in a grateful gasp of air and realised that he was going to be ok.

Like an Olympian who has just finished an arduous marathon, he gulped in the air desperately. He put his hands out to either side and continued to take in monstrous breaths.

"I'm really sorry I had to do that," said Varuna.

"How ... can ... I ... hear ... you ... underwater?" panted the Captain.

"You're covered in a mermaid's breath. It means you can breathe underwater and acclimatise to the sea temperature. It also means that you can hear the person who covered you in it. I'm sorry – you must have been scared, and confused," admitted Varuna.

He was getting his breath back and he could feel the bubble warming up to body temperature.

Varuna continued, "I'm so sorry I had to drag you so far down, but I couldn't risk being seen by your friend. My cover would have been blown! I've been following you since the harbour. You're not mad at me, are you?"

Just happy that he wasn't going to drown, Culbert replied, "Well, as it turns out you're not trying to kill me ... no, I'm not mad."

"I've been thinking about you," said Varuna bashfully.

"Really?" Culbert failed to hide his surprise.

"Yes, now come on, Culbert McFinn – let me take you to where I'm from. I have a lot to show you."

She reached into the bubble and held his hand as they began to descend further into the Fijian depths.

Marvin was slumped on the deck of the boat, his voice

hoarse from shouting all afternoon and his eyes red with crying. He held his head in his hands, distraught.

"I'm so sorry, Culbert. This is all my fault. If I hadn't been so greedy you'd still be here ..." Another great sob escaped.

The sun was setting quickly over the horizon and the sea air was beginning to cool. After hours searching for Culbert, Marvin had concluded with a heavy heart that he would have to go home and tell the islanders what had happened – and raise a search party for the Captain.

His plastic bounty now seemed a hollow prize if it meant losing a good friend.

Crestfallen, he started the ignition of the Flying Fox. There was no time to lose.

Marvin worked the little boat hard, knowing that Culbert's chances of surviving grew smaller as each moment passed. The engines rumbled. It was now a race against time to get back to Maloto and fetch aid for his friend.

CHAPTER 6

A PLEA FOR HELP...AND A
TALKING TAXI

S wimming further into the emerald depths, Culbert and Varuna looked up at the bottom of Marvin's boat. Culbert watched in horror as Marvin weighed anchor and the engines started up.

"He's going without me!" said the Captain in astonishment.

"Don't worry, he's probably heading back to Maloto to tell the rest of the islanders that you're lost at sea."

"But I'm not lost! We have to tell Marvin that I'm ok! He'll be worried sick!" He let go of Varuna's hand and started to swim up toward the surface.

Varuna pulled back on his hand. "I'm so sorry, but you can't do that."

Disconcerted, Culbert responded, "Why on Earth not?"

She gave him a choice. "Look, you can swim back up to Marvin, with a slim chance that he will see you and all will be well – but if you go up to the surface and tell him what happened, then there's a very high chance that he will also see me, and expose the secrets that my people have been trying to hide for thousands of years." Culbert felt her hand trembling as it held his wrist.

He slowed briefly, listening to Varuna as she continued.

"We watch humans every day, repeatedly destroying our rivers and oceans, dumping their poisonous waste and plastic into the water without a care for those of us who live here, needlessly harvesting creatures for food and consumption – and killing everything else. Even now, we're swimming in a shroud of plastic, and it's getting worse. I know your friend is cleaning some of it up, but he's just one man, Culbert. What can he do, really?" She paused, her eyes filled with despair. "I just can't take the risk of being discovered, though – we Lapatians have gone undetected for thousands of years and we want to keep it that way. We need your help."

"But why me? I'm a human ... if you're generalising, then I'm just like all the rest ... aren't I?" As he spoke, Culbert looked up again and saw the wake of Marvin's boat fanning into the distance. He'd gone.

"But you're not, Culbert," said Varuna. "You're not like the rest at all. You love the ocean and you reuse items that most would just throw away. We've been watching you for a long time, Culbert McFinn. I must confess that our meeting that night wasn't a coincidence. I was asked to come and get you.

"You care about the seas and our environment. You teach all the islanders about the importance of keeping the seas clean and not overfishing our waters – and you've got the whole island reusing plastic for different purposes rather than just chucking it in the sea.

"We need your help, Culbert, we're losing the fight. I want you to meet with my kin. We think that with your help we can work out a way to teach the rest of the world about how close we are to killing all the fish, molluscs, crustaceans and mammals who call the sea their home. Dakuwaga would be proud!"

The Captain took one final glance up to the surface, just in case Marvin's boat had returned. It hadn't. He sighed and started to swim with Varuna again.

"Please forgive me, Marvin," he said. "It sounds like my services are in greater demand elsewhere." Culbert turned to Varuna. "So when can I go home?"

She held both of his hands. "Soon, I promise. Your disappearance will draw too much immediate sea traffic and unwanted attention so you'll need to stay hidden for a while, but I swear on my forefathers that I will bring you back to Maloto so you can explain to Marvin."

Varuna led the Captain into the deep, skirting along the top of the reefs. The deeper they swam, the bigger the fishes grew. They passed close by a group of reef sharks who all seemed undeterred by their presence – they were more interested in skimming the reef looking for their daily feed of smaller fish in the nooks and crannies.

The reef was abundant and vibrant with life, truly a spectacle to be seen. Culbert had seen reefs before, of course – there weren't many he hadn't seen – but none as bright and colourful as this was. No wonder they called it the Purple Wall. It was an enormous barrier that separated Maloto from the other Fijian islands with a dense layer of soft coral trees, whips and sea fans.

He noticed that a large part of the reef was white.

He pointed in horror. "Blackbeard's ghost, what's happening to the reef, Varuna? Is it dead?"

"Well, that's what you humans call bleaching. It happens when the water becomes too warm."

"Kraken's tentacles. That's awful," said Culbert.

Varuna pointed at the reef. "When the water gets too warm, the coral expels the algae living inside it, and it turns completely white. But all is not lost. Not all of the coral is dead," she continued. "We can save it, but we need to act soon or it will be too late. That's why you must help us, Culbert. The oceans are dying. You can see it with your own eyes."

Shocked and saddened, Culbert bowed his head in shame. He took one final glance at the coral before continuing to follow Varuna.

Culbert looked at her and smiled, although thoughts of Marvin played on his mind. It felt like they had been swimming for an age and the waters were becoming darker still. Shards of sunlight were beaming through the water but the Captain knew that they would have to find refuge soon as darkness was coming – and that meant feeding time.

Similarly conscious that time wasn't on their side, Varuna slowed, paused and looked around. "Hmm," she said, "we're being hunted.'

She reached down to grab a large empty whelk shell – *Cabestana spengleri*, if he wasn't mistaken – which was tied to her waist. She unhooked it and blew into the point, resulting in a lot of fizzes and bubbles emanating from the larger end.

"In the name of Long John's parrot, what are you doing?"

"We've got a long way to go still. Night is drawing near, and so are the predators of the deep. I'm getting us a cab, of course!" said Varuna.

"A cab? What the ...?"

"Just stop there and wait."

Out of the murky blue depths, the Captain saw a shadow that looked like a torpedo flying toward him at a rate of knots. He couldn't quite make out what it was. He turned to Varuna.

"Er, we've got something coming at us very, very quickly ..." he said, flapping his arm in the direction of the missile.

Varuna didn't respond but let go of his hand. "What are you doing?"

He looked more closely at the object that was approaching. "My word, I haven't seen one of those in a while!"

A dusky dolphin flew into view, spinning and pirouetting in the waters around him. The Captain puffed out his cheeks. "Phew ... thought I was a goner there!"

"This is Dusty," said Varuna.

"'Allo, Varuna, you rang? 'Aven't seen you in these parts for a few months – you need a lift, love?"

"Actually, yes, if you don't mind, Dusty. We're still a bit of a way from home." She pointed at the Captain. "This is Culbert McFinn."

"G'day, Finny," said Dusty, nodding his beak.

"H-h-hello. So your name is Dusty ...?"

"Yep," replied Dusty, "fastest taxi in all the Pacific!"

"Your name is Dusty, and you're a dusky dolphin ..."

"Last time I checked, I was, mate," Dusty retorted.

"And you don't find that funny?" smiled Culbert.

"Funny?"

"Dusty the dusky dolphin ..."

"Nope, don't find that funny at all, mate. Although what I would find funny, if I were you, is that you're having a conversation with a dolphin and you think the oddest thing is his name. That's bloody hilarious!"

Culbert, realising the truth in this, looked straight at Varuna with a start.

"Don't worry" she said, "it's the bubble – you're not hearing things or going mad. Just grab a hold of his dorsal fin and hang on tight."

"So, where to, Varuna love?"

"Take us home. Take us back to Lapatia."

"Righto, will do. Hang on tight, mate – I'm not going to

hang about, it's getting dark and I flew past some very unsavoury-looking characters a few miles back. They looked bloomin' 'ungry, too ..."

CHAPTER 7
THE CURSE OF KADAVU

Varuna and the Captain both clung on to Dusty's dorsal fin. Dusty let out a volley of high-pitched clicks and he was off. Like a silver bullet, he was zipping due north toward Samoa.

Culbert had to squint to see where they were going, but they were travelling so fast that he couldn't make out anything he recognised.

Dusty, like all good taxi drivers, turned to the Captain for a chat.

"So, first time to Lapatia, then?"

The Captain was still too bemused to talk, so he just nodded.

Dusty took that as a cue to continue his patter.

"Well, my lad, you're in for a treat. Ancient legend has it that the kingdom known as Lapatia was once protected by the sea guardian known as Lapoto.

"Now, he was part man, part barracuda, and he guarded the island and the Lapatians who lived there.

"Lapoto was a huge fella, stood eleven feet tall, all neck and teeth, he was. One of the good guys. He protected the people of Lapatia, made sure they had safe passage to the mainland, Lapatia was peaceful and serene under the rule of Lapoto. Fascinating stuff, history, innit?

"Where was I ...? Oh yeah. But anyway, there was one ancient sea guardian whose intentions were not as pure and honest as the others and his greed and jealousy made him want to claim all of the Fijian and Samoan islands for his own domain. There's always one, eh?

"He started with the Northern Islands of Fiji, working his way down the coast slaying all that stood in his path, claiming all the small islands for himself, and sinking the other islands that didn't cooperate.

"His name was Kadavu: part man, part shark. Stood over twenty feet tall with a mouth full of razor-sharp teeth and eyes darker than an onyx stone."

Culbert was listening intently to the story. Although he had heard these tales many times from his grandfather, this time they seemed real and the dolphin's enthusiasm was infectious.

"You still listening?" asked Dusty, turning his head without slowing.

"Of course. Please, carry on," said Culbert.

"Well, Kadavu wanted Lapatia all for himself, you see, so he challenged Lapoto and there was an epic battle.

"The two fought majestically for days, ceaselessly slamming each other into the Lapatian landscape. The great Lapoto was defeated and Lapatia was Kadavu's to claim – but the guardians' fighting had caused the land to splinter and break free from the mainland. Lapatia was cast adrift.

"Not wanting to lose their homeland, the courageous Lapatian people rallied, and with all their might they managed to ward off the fearsome Kadavu, sending him back to the ocean.

"But this only enraged him further. If he couldn't have the

island for himself, then no other sea guardian should have it. So he plunged his trident deep into the heart of the island. Unstable, it began to sink.

"This was too much for many villagers and they began to flee the island. Those who stayed had to learn new ways of surviving in their new environment.

"As the island slowly sank to the ocean floor, the Lapatians became desperate to work out how they could survive and adapt to their new environment. The remaining few villagers prayed for mercy to Poseidon.

"Taking pity on them, Poseidon granted all the remaining villagers scales, tails and fins so they could adapt to living under the sea.

"Forever grateful for their new-found abilities, the Lapatians vowed to Poseidon to keep his oceans clean and free from war, and ever since then the agreement has been kept. Until now."

Varuna held Culbert's hand. "The Lapatians are the shepherds of the sea. We all originated from Lapatia, but we are all over the world's oceans, keeping our rivers, seas and oceans safe. But over the last hundred years we've started losing the fight."

"That's right!" interrupted Dusty. "Humans are dumping so much rubbish into the seas, the Lapatians just can't keep up!"

"We can't do it on our own any more," blurted Varuna. "That's why I found you, Culbert. That's why I'm bringing you back to Lapatia. You're going to help us find a way to clean up the oceans for good!"

"I will help you, my love," said Culbert, squeezing her hand.

"You do realise that you're in the presence of royalty, mate?" Dusty said.

Culbert turned to Varuna. "Royalty?"

"She's the daughter of the king of Lapatia. Her great great great great grandad fought alongside Lapoto to keep Kadavu at bay."

"Why don't you approach humans?" asked Culbert.

"Kadavu cursed us all. Humans think that we're monsters and only those who have the divine sight can see us. So we hide. For centuries we've hidden from the human race, but on the rare occasion, humans would spot a Lapatian bathing on the top of a reef or in a cove when the tide was out," said Varuna.

"I reckon this is really quite an honour, then, being taken to their kingdom." Dusty winked at Culbert.

"Is all of that true?" said the Captain humbly to Varuna.

"Yes, all of it. We need your help, Culbert: not only is the rubbish becoming overwhelming, but we hear things ..."

"What type of things?" asked Culbert, confused.

"Some believe that Kadavu is due to return. It's written in the ancient sea runes that the marked child will bring of his return." She bit her lip.

Dusty had nothing more to say. He simply swam faster.

CHAPTER 8
MARVIN & MARILLA

Marvin tapped on the fuel gauge, but the needle didn't move. It was on the red and the engine was starting to splutter, but the harbour was in sight. "Come on, old girl. Just get me back to the harbour, I'll fix you up when we get there," he said, tapping the tiller for encouragement.

The little boat chugged on.

The Flying Fox was running on fumes but the harbour walls were drawing closer.

As the boat entered the harbour, Marvin sounded the horn to alert fellow fisherman and sailors who were going about their business, working on their boats and lobster pots. He slowed the Flying Fox and pulled in. The boat was almost at a standstill as he heard the engine conk out. Pppfffttt ... BANG!

But he'd made it. "Help! Help! Listen to me! I need your help, all of you!" Marvin shouted to the onlookers, waving his arms frantically.

He quickly threw the anchor overboard and chucked the gangplank down. Before it had chance to settle, he ran across it onto the harbour. Somebody caught his eye: a tall, willowy woman he had never seen before. He ran off the gangplank past her, almost knocking her over.

"Sorry!" he shouted over his shoulder to the stranger. "No time to lose!"

"No problem, Marvin!" she said, bowing in his direction.

Perturbed by the stranger but not deviating from the important task at hand, he kept running, straight into the Dolphin Tavern. He burst through the door.

"Help! Help! Culbert is lost at sea – I need to raise a rescue team quickly, who's with me?" he bellowed.

The bustle and hum of rowdy chatter drained away and the tavern fell deathly silent. All eyes turned around to look at him.

He waited for a response, but nobody said a word. He tried again. "Will anybody help me? Culbert! Culbert McFinn, the Captain! He's in serious peril! Come on! He's done so much for you lot, and now he needs your help!"

The silence persisted. Everyone seemed to be looking at something over his shoulder.

He turned around. The mysterious stranger had followed him into the tavern. She was tall and slender, her skin was pale and drawn, and she wore a deep purple cloak. "Hello, Marvin. My name is Marilla," she said in a silky voice. She smiled and bowed her head in his direction, never changing her gaze, like a tiger fixed on an antelope, waiting for the right time to pounce.

Confused, he shook his head. "What's going on? How do you know my name? We need to help Culbert now!"

The mention of Culbert seemed to trigger her into action. She raised her finger toward Marvin. "Seize him!"

The rabble rose from their seats and started to approach Marvin. Two slack-jawed yobs grabbed him, holding his arms tight.

His utter confusion was turning quickly into desperate fear.

"Wh ... what's happening?" he said.

"Shh ..." Marilla put her finger over her lips. "You'll wish you'd never come back, my fat little friend."

One of the vagabonds holding his arm quickly tied Marvin's hands together with rope. He grabbed an old dish-cloth off the bar and stuffed it in his mouth. Marvin gagged.

"There you go, Mistress," grunted the wretch.

She nodded in appreciation and turned to address the whole rabble.

"The island is now under my command!" she laughed. "I have come a long way and waited a very long time, but Maloto will soon belong to its rightful owner."

Marvin tussled, trying to free himself. He attempted to speak but all he could muster was a few muffled dribbles.

Marilla moved threateningly close to him. "So, you're friends with the infamous Culbert McFinn, are you?" she sneered.

He said nothing.

"Come now, you needn't play dumb, my little pot-bellied pig." She slapped the side of his face. "I know you are. You've known him for a long time, have you not?"

Again, Marvin said nothing.

"But do you really know him? What of his background? Where is he really from? What's his lineage?"

Marvin said nothing, but continued to stare at Marilla, beads of sweat beginning to trickle down his brow.

Well you see, Marvin, Culbert is a direct descendant of the foul octopus god Dakuwaga, whom you all hold in such high regard, and I need him. More importantly, I need his blood — his very essence — to bring back our Dark Lord so he can control these waters once again. As for you, Marvin, well, you will be our latest sacrifice to the Midnight Marauders."

Marvin's heart sank. He had heard stories about the ruthless Midnight Marauders, who dwelt deep in the Maloto forest. He'd always hoped that they weren't true. Legend had it that the Midnight Marauders were a tribe of savages who were the very first islanders on Maloto. Some said that they helped Dakuwaga to banish Kadavu back to the salty depths. Others believed them to be cannibals.

Marilla squeezed Marvin's chubby face.

"Yes, that's right, my portly pal — you should look scared! My chunky little fellow, they will be so pleased to feast on you!"

Marvin stood firm.

Marilla sighed and nodded to the ruffians guarding him. "Very well, take him to the forest. Let the Midnight Marauders do what they wish with him. I will find Culbert myself!"

With that, the two unsavoury ragamuffins manhandled Marvin out of the tavern and marched him away from the harbour to the forests at the foot of the Mulgar Mountains.

CHAPTER 9

THE VILLAGE UNDER THE SEA

Dusty turned around to speak to the pair. "Not far now gang, won't be long. Just over this next reef."

Culbert couldn't see. He could hardly open his eyes. As courageous as he was, this was beginning to scare him a little and he let out a little whimper. He wanted this journey to end. "I can't believe I'm going to say this — but are we there yet, Dusty? I'm losing my grip!"

"Yep, we're here." Dusty started to slow ... then jolted and came to an abrupt stop. His two passengers shot forward; Varuna naturally came to a gentle flowing stop, whereas Culbert arched over the sea bed and landed in a sandbank a good thirty metres away, like a boulder fired from a catapult. A plume of sand exploded with a whoomph, creating a wall of beige and making it impossible to see where he had landed.

Varuna called out "Culbert? Are you OK, my love?" She was concerned he might have burst his bubble.

Scrambling to his feet, coughing and spluttering, he caught his breath and squinted through the thick sand clouds. "Yes. Yes, I'm fine."

He heard Dusty's voice through the haze. "Great to meet

with you, Captain Culbert McFinn. Varuna, darlin', it's always a pleasure of course, send my love to the family."

With that he let out a number of clicks and screeches and zipped away.

"Thanks, Dusty, see you again soon, I hope!" spluttered Culbert.

Varuna came to find him through the haze. "You're always falling over around me, Culbert McFinn," she smiled.

As the sand cleared in front of him he couldn't quite focus at first, but then the view sharpened and he was awestruck at what he saw. In front of him was the most beautiful fishing village he had ever seen.

He shook his head and looked again. The sand was thinning further and he could see more clearly. Yes – this was an underwater village. All the houses were covered with all manner of crustaceans, barnacles, starfish and hermit crabs, with coral, kelp and seaweed gently flowing on the ocean's current like scraggly green flags from chimney tops and roofs.

All the house doors and windows had been removed. Culbert supposed there was no need for them as there was unlikely to be bad weather at the bottom of the ocean. Varuna had told him that the Lapatians were peaceful, honest people and he assumed crime was an uncommon occurrence.

Thick underwater reeds mapped out the roads, where dozens of Lapatians were going about their daily business. It was a thriving little village, just like on the land, although these people had fish tails.

Varuna reached into the bubble and took Culbert's hand. "Come with me, my love, and meet with my kin."

The Captain turned to her. "This place is even more magical than I imagined! It's just like home, but more ... under the sea?"

"It's time to come and meet my family, Culbert, will you

come with me?" She pulled on his hand lovingly and gestured for him to follow her.

He nodded. "Let's meet your kin. Teach me all about Lapatia. Oh, I can't wait to tell all the folks back on Maloto about this!"

Varuna stopped. "No. You must never tell anyone about Lapatia, Culbert. Our secret has stayed hidden for millennia and we intend to keep it that way!"

"OK – but when will I be going home?" asked Culbert. The excitement had gone from his voice.

"This is your new home, Culbert. We need you here. I need you. We're losing the fight!"

Culbert looked at the wondrous village before him, and thought briefly about the life he would be leaving behind. And Marvin – poor Marvin ... "OK, but on one condition. I'm here for no longer than a week. I need to get back and make sure Marvin is OK. Then I'll come back and learn the ways of Lapatia."

"Of course. I promise that you're only here for a week and then we will go back to Maloto and you can check on Marvin."

CHAPTER 10
ENTER DYLAN AND AXNEUS

Almost fourteen years had passed since the Captain had disappeared from his beloved waters of Maloto to be taken to Lapatia by Varuna.

In the first few weeks after his disappearance, Varuna kept her promise and took Culbert back to see Marvin – only to find that he was nowhere to be seen. They went to the harbour and found the Flying Fox moored up. Culbert checked the lighthouse; no sign, he couldn't even see Adrian. The lighthouse was deserted, and it hadn't been in operation since Culbert left. Things didn't seem right.

He asked the villagers where Marvin might have gone, only to be met with silence, ill-informed suggestions and dead ends.

Crestfallen, Culbert returned to Lapatia with Varuna, and with nothing more to go back for (apart from Adrian, whose sarcastic remarks he could easily live without) he threw himself into a new life.

Culbert and Varuna were married in a spectacular under-water ceremony by the high priestess of Lapatia.

Varuna taught him about the history of Lapatia and he

became integrated into its culture, even learning the native tongue. He learned to hunt with the local Lapatian sea warriors, and in return he showed them how to catch more rubbish with his ingenious inventions.

Time seems to stand still underwater. Days turned into weeks; the weeks rolled into months; and the years took care of themselves.

Life was good, but the Captain did always yearn to return to Maloto one day. He missed his lighthouse, he missed his friends and the villagers and most of all he missed Marvin. Adrian – well, not so much.

Besides which, he had other company these days. Culbert and Varuna had become four.

Their younger son, Axneus, was almost ten. He was neat and tidy, scrawny, with chestnut brown hair, brown eyes and a very strong likeness to his mother. He found it hard to make genuine friends as, despite Culbert's efforts to teach him, he didn't like to share.

Unlike his older brother, Axneus was more interested in looking for treasure, possessions and shiny things. He always craved being the centre of attention and cared deeply about what other people thought of him, often to the point where he would say or do anything to make himself look better in the eyes of his peers. This resulted in him having lots of hangers-on, for all the wrong reasons, but very few real friends.

Dylan, the older brother, was fast approaching his thirteenth birthday. Dylan was confident and charismatic. He had wavy blond hair and dark green eyes.

Dylan was never interested in possessions and found knowledge and learning a much more powerful currency than money and things.

He loved to listen to his dad's stories about the terrible way that humans treated the oceans and, like his dad, was always keen to help others. He had his dad's keen eye for inventing and designing things, too.

Although both boys were half Lapatian, they looked completely human, with no sign of their mother's tail, scales or fins.

From birth, both had been encapsulated in a bubble by Varuna as she didn't want to take the risk of them drowning, not knowing if they would survive underwater.

Being different from everybody else inevitably set the two brothers up for some teasing and ridicule from their schoolmates.

Dylan knew his own mind; he only judged people by the content of their character, and made solid friendships with only a few who shared the same views as him. He was confident enough in his outlook that the teasing didn't bother him.

Axneus, on the other hand, took the teasing and the jeers to heart and plotted his revenge every time he was met with a challenge. Instead of letting go of the silly comments, he wallowed in bitterness, making him very insecure and unable to hold on to friendships for long.

It was morning, and the school bell had just rung for the first lesson. The hallway was bustling with life as pupils hurried around trying to get to their first lesson.

"Oi, bubble brain!" shouted a low-browed bully boy in the hallway.

Axneus chose to ignore him. This only goaded the bully further and he rifled through Axneus's locker. He picked up a modern history textbook on Lapatia and hurled it in Axneus's direction. "Hey, bubble boy! You're History!"

With impeccable timing, the book smacked Axneus square on the back of the head and he tumbled to the hard, unforgiving floor. Before Axneus had time to react, the whole hallway exploded with laughter, whistles and shouting.

"Who threw that?" screamed Axneus into the sea of nameless faces.

"Enjoy the trip!" another faceless goon shouted.

"Yeah, very funny. Mark my words, I will have my vengeance!" Axneus took off his backpack and took out a small notepad covered in names. "You just made the list." He scribbled the culprit's name down furiously and underlined it with his permanent marker.

Dylan sat gazing out of his classroom window, waiting for the bell to ring. He was watching seahorses playing in the reeds of sea kelp swaying in the gentle current ... and not paying any attention at all to the maths lesson that was continuing outside of his daydream.

"*Pssst ... psst,*" Dylan heard behind him.

Murdoch passed a note forward. Dylan quickly grabbed it and opened it under his desk without Mrs Pike-Teeth seeing it.

It read, *Happy birthday Bubble Boy!*

This was the name that Murdoch had called Dylan all the way through growing up. Murdoch now slapped him on the back.

"Thanks, Murdoch," whispered Dylan.

Murdoch and Dylan had been friends since they were little, Murdoch came from a great line of Lapatian sea warriors whose descendants helped defend the Lapatians from Kadavu centuries ago.

Murdoch replied, "So, what you doing for the big one-three?"

"My dad's taking me and my brother to where he used to live. We're off to Maloto, for a camping trip. I can't wait!" he whispered.

"Dylan! Murdoch!" shouted Mrs Pike-Teeth. "Why is it always you two interrupting the class? Don't you want to learn about long division?" she snapped.

"Sorry, Mrs Pike-Teeth," the two said simultaneously.

Almost on cue the bell rang for the end of school. The classroom erupted and everybody started to get their belongings together and head for home.

"Now remember, class: you all have homework for tomorrow on the Great Barrier Reef."

Nobody was paying attention as they all fled from the boredom of their long division class, which was already becoming a faded memory.

Dylan walked out with Murdoch and they were promptly met by Narissa. Murdoch had a secret crush on her but, like most boys at that age, he didn't understand the feeling so he expressed his affection with an occasional punch on her arm. It seemed to do the trick.

"Hey, Narissa," mumbled Murdoch, as he slapped her on the back.

Narissa stumbled forward with the force. She thought Murdoch was a bit strange. Recovering her balance and taking no notice of him, she waved to Dylan.

"Hi, Dylan! Happy birthday for tomorrow," she said excitedly as the three walked out of the school gates and began to make their way home.

Murdoch butted in before Dylan could speak. "Hello, Narissa ... er, nice hair. Did you grow it yourself?"

Dylan and Narissa both stopped, looked straight at Murdoch, and burst into fits of laughter.

Murdoch looked hurt and confused. "Why are you laughing? Stop laughing at me." Murdoch was destined to be a legendary warrior, but he had a sensitive side.

Dylan tried to suppress his laughter. "We're not laughing at you, buddy – it was just funny, what you said."

Narissa backed him up. "Yes, it just made us laugh, we're not laughing at you." She reached out and touched Murdoch's arm. Instantly he stopped pouting and started to calm down.

"So, Murdoch tells me you're off camping on Maloto tonight?" said Narissa, turning back to Dylan.

"Yeah. Me, Dad and my brother are going. Don't know how we're going to get there," shrugged Dylan.

"Have you heard much about Maloto?" asked Narissa.

"Well, only what my dad has told me. He said that it's a magical place, full of kind-hearted people who care about the environment and the ocean, and—"

"So you haven't heard about the mysterious happenings on the island?"

"No. He hasn't talked about anything like that!" said Dylan.

"I'm sure it's just a silly rumour, nothing more ..."

Dylan looked a little perturbed by this, and asked her to elaborate.

Narissa continued. "Maloto used to be such a beautiful place, but over the last ten years the island has been cursed and under the control of a sea nymph. She has all of the villagers under a spell and they do exactly what she commands ..."

Narissa put out her arms like a zombie and rocked from foot to foot.

Dylan's worried frown soon turned to laughter. "Stop being so silly, Narissa!" He swiped away her mocking advances.

She quickly broke character. "Oh, this is me! I nearly forgot where I was. Having so much fun!" she said, pointing to her road. "Bye, Dylan, have a great birthday, tell me all about it next week at school."

Dylan nodded and waved. "I will. See you back at school."

"I'll walk you home, Narissa," shouted Murdoch. He waved hurriedly at Dylan and ran off, following Narissa home. "Have a good birthday, bubble boy!" he yelled over his shoulder.

Left alone, Dylan allowed his mind to wander back to the forthcoming adventure of his camping trip.

He was musing on what Narissa had said when a stone bounced off his bubble. BOINK.

He turned around quickly. "Hey! Watch out!" It was Axneus.

"Haha! Bubble boy! I like that! I'm going to use that as your new nickname!" sneered Axneus.

"You're in a bubble too, snot-for-brains," replied Dylan.

"Yes, but mine's different to yours."

"Fine," said Dylan dismissively. "Well in that case, why don't I race you home?"

Dylan took off like a rocket and ran home.

"Hey! Wait up! That's cheating!" spluttered Axneus as he failed to catch up with his brother.

"Last one home's a rotten sea-turtle's egg!" shouted Dylan.

CHAPTER 11
DYLAN'S BIRTHDAY

The two brothers burst into the kitchen and were greeted by the Captain, who was preparing for Dylan's birthday present. Culbert had always promised to take them both to Maloto on Dylan's thirteenth birthday to show them where he used to live.

"Slow down, you two! And gather round. As I promised, I'm taking you to Maloto – and I have a few ground rules before we set off," said the Captain sternly. "You must keep quiet when we're on the island. Do not speak to anyone on the island. You must hold on tight to the taxi—"

Axneus interrupted him. "Will there be treasure, Dad?"

"Depends what you class as treasure, son."

"You know. Pirate treasure. Gold, doubloons, crowns, rings – stuff like that."

"No, Ax, nothing like that. Or at least, if there is, I haven't found it, and I've spent many a long day fishing in those waters ..."

"Shame. I'd look amazing in a crown."

Dylan rolled his eyes and ignored Axneus's comment. He listened as their dad continued.

"It's extremely important that we are not spotted by any of the islanders. We must stay out of the water after dark – some hungry nasties patrol those waters when the sun sets. We'll hide out at Neptune's Tower – that's if my old friend Rusty remembers me."

"Who's Rusty, Dad?" said Dylan.

"Rusty is my oldest friend. He runs Neptune's Tower, one of the oldest taverns on the island. The tower is reputed to hold magical powers and only a few people know its where-abouts. Luckily for you two, your old dad is one of them!" He shot the pair a wink and tapped his nose. "The building itself is hundreds of feet tall and completely covered in gold. It's quite a sight."

"Gold!" piped up Axneus, "now you're talking!"

Dylan and Culbert ignored him.

Varuna swam into the kitchen and joined the boys. "Right, boys, I've called for Dusty. He'll be here in five minutes."

"Now, you're both in those bubbles at the moment, but they will pop as soon as you reach the surface. You'll be able to breathe on land but it will take a bit of adjusting." She handed them both something green and slimy.

"Chew on this. When you're in the water, begin to blow and a bubble will form. All you need to do is step into it and you can breathe underwater again for the trip home."

The boys looked scornfully at the handfuls of vegetation they had been given. Varuna continued, "It's forest samphire. It's extremely rare and found only in the underwater forests of Lapatia. Just chew it. You'll know when you can start to blow as it will turn rubbery."

Next, she unfastened her necklace. It was made from a rare seaweed that was bound together tightly and wrapped around a tooth that was broken at its base. "Take this, Dylan.

It will keep you all safe," ordered Varuna as she fastened it carefully around Dylan's neck.

"I won't take it off, Mum, I promise!"

"See that you don't," smiled Varuna.

She turned to the Captain. "You be careful back on Maloto, Culbert. Make sure the boys aren't seen – and you bring them back safely."

"Yes, dear," said Culbert flippantly with a wave of his hand. "They'll be fine."

With that they heard a collection of clicks and screeches, and looked out of the window to investigate. Culbert handed each of the boys a small black pebble and told them to hold it. Their taxi was here.

A silvery shadow appeared in the doorway. "G'day guys, it's been a bloody long time since I've seen you two, how the de—" Dusty stopped himself mid-sentence as he noticed the boys.

"Well, hold on a minute – what do we have here?" Dusty swam through the front door then gently closer to the pair. "Well, stuff yer finger in my blowhole, who are you two?"

Dylan looked in amazement at his dad. "I can understand him!"

"Yes, that's a little present from me. It's called the fish tongue stone. When you're holding it you can talk to sea creatures."

"H … hello. My name's Dylan, and this is my younger brother Axneus."

"A pleasure to meet you both, I'm sure." Dusty performed a flamboyant spin and took a bow. "Dusty the dusky dolphin, at your service."

The boys sniggered at the tongue-tying title.

"See, I told you your name was funny!" said Culbert as he went to give Dusty a hug. "Good to see you, old friend. What's the traffic like?"

"Good as gold, cuz. Be wise to get moving though, so rattle yer dags!"

"Right, boys, you heard Dusty. Time to get moving. Give your mother a kiss goodbye and let's set sail. Next stop: adventure!"

The boys let out a jubilant cheer, gathered their belongings, secured their satchels over their shoulders and gave their mother a kiss and a hug before bounding out of the front door.

Culbert blew his beloved a kiss. "We'll be back by sunrise tomorrow. I'm taking them to see Rusty and we'll camp on the beach overnight. We won't be spotted."

"See you tomorrow, my darling." Varuna caught the kiss and held it to her chest.

"Right, hold on to Dusty's dorsal fin, boys. Hold on tight – this is going to be quite an experience, I can assure you!"

Culbert checked the boys were holding on and gave Dusty a tap on his side to give him the green light.

"All aboard!! We'll be there in a few shakes of a lamb's tail!"

And with that, Dusty shot off like a torpedo.

"WOAHHH!!" the boys wailed ... and held on for dear life.

"Next stop will be the warm waters of Maloto Island, keep your arms and legs inside the vehicle at all times, make sure all items of luggage is safely stored in the overhead lockers," chortled Dusty.

Skipping through the water, the four zipped along like a rocket, but in his haste, Axneus hadn't closed his satchel properly and the knot he'd thrown together was quickly coming loose ... His bag opened up and out whipped the forest samphire, only to disappear into the deep blue behind them. Axneus noticed this, but his dad and Dylan didn't, so he kept quiet and continued to hold on tight to Dusty's dorsal fin.

"So, I hear it's somebody's birthday?" said Dusty, completely unaware of what had just happened.

"YES! ... it's MINE!!" screeched Dylan as he tried to hold on.

"How old are you then? Twenty-four, twenty-five?" joked Dusty.

"No, silly. Thirteen." Dylan rolled his eyes at the back of Dusty's sleek head.

"I see. A young 'un. So yer dad's taking you to see his home town then, is he?"

They were travelling far too fast for Dylan to lift his head up to talk any more, so he just nodded.

"Eh?" said Dusty. "Can't hear you, cuz. These lugholes ain't as young as they used ter be."

The Captain spoke for Dylan. "Yes. I'm taking the boys back to Neptune's Tower, and my old lighthouse."

"A rare treat, I might add. Has yer dad told you about the mysteries around Neptune's Tower?" said Dusty as they zipped along.

The two boys nodded.

"Well, keep holding on tight, cuz. I don't want to lose a passenger ... again."

Dylan looked over to his brother who was now looking a little bit scared. The two gripped the fin for dear life.

"Mind you, mate, a lot's changed since yer left all those years ago. The lighthouse has been left abandoned, by all accounts, and sometimes the island is covered in a foul-smelling mist. All the villagers have got aggressive, selfish and rude, so they say. Not very nice to be around. Not like in your day, eh?

"There's a really nasty sea nymph running the show there now, so be careful. And Marvin ... well, Marvin took your disappearance hard. He went to take out a rescue party but he didn't make it, for some reason ...

"The last I heard was that he'd been eaten by the Midnight Marauders. Real shame, I used to swim alongside his boats some days and eat the leftover sea flies he threw over the side of the boat."

Dylan struggled to lift up his head against the streaming water to ask a question. "What's a sea fly, Dad?"

"It's what us seafaring folk call shrimps, due to them eating all the rubbish off the sea bed."

Dylan nodded with intent but couldn't manage to speak further.

Culbert turned to Axneus. "Ax, you OK? You're very quiet over there!"

Axneus passed up another opportunity to tell his dad about his mishap. "Just trying to hold on tight, Dad!"

"Do you know any more about what's been happening on the island, Dusty?" said the Captain.

"Not really ... that bloody bird's still living in the light-house, though."

"What – Adrian?"

"Yeah, that's the blighter – he stole a herring out of my mouth once. Swooped straight in and pinched it, little swine!"

"Yes ... that sounds like par for the course," sighed Culbert.

The four zipped through the Samoan waves, quickly moving into Fijian waters. The Captain could feel that he was nearing home, he could feel it in the waters. The ocean seemed to change colour from a deep sapphire blue to a soft turquoise.

He spotted a number of familiar reefs in the distance. "We're getting closer, boys" he said, smiling.

"So what's the plan, cuz?" said Dusty.

"I'm going to have to go straight to Neptune's Tower, to make sure we're not spotted. Do you know where that is?"

Dusty laughed. "Of course I do, mate. Wouldn't be much of a taxi if I didn't, would I? But you won't be able to go there straight away – it won't be dusk for another hour or so."

"Oh, Haddock's hellfire!!" said the Captain. "OK, well what about dropping us in the salt marshes? We'll have to hide in the dunes until dusk."

"Sure thing, Cap, won't be long now."

The waters were becoming lighter and shallower; they were getting near to Maloto. "How much longer?" said Axneus impatiently.

"Another couple of clicks, little one, we're nearly there. Just need to be careful where we drop you."

"I don't care. I'm bored now and my arms are getting tired," moaned Axneus.

"Just be patient," said Dylan, "we won't be much longer. Just think of all the exciting things we're going to see!"

CHAPTER 12
LEARNING TO WALK

Dusty slowed down as they approached the mouth of the estuary leading to the salt marshes. The sand was brilliant white and the water was a soft turquoise. Below them huge lumps of sea kelp and seaweed swayed in the gentle current.

"I'm going to slip through this seaweed, gents. You won't be spotted, I can assure you."

Dusty dipped into the forest of seaweed at barely more than walking pace. Still holding on gently, the boys relaxed and caught their breath.

"I won't be able to go right up the estuary, lads – I could get beached. But you can just slip through the seaweed and swim up the estuary until you reach the salt marshes."

Culbert reached out and cupped his hand around an unsuspecting little sprat. He slipped it into Dusty's mouth. "Thanks, Dusty. Always a superior service," he said, gently tapping Dusty's side.

"Right, boys, let go and move into the seaweed. I'll give you a call tomorrow, Dusty. Pick up from here, OK?"

"Sure thing, mate. Lovely to meet you, boys! Thanks for

travelling with Dusty Tours and I'll see you tomorrow. Have fun!"

The boys thanked Dusty – one sincerely, the other sarcastically – let go of his fin and drifted into the thick seaweed on the sea bed. The Captain followed.

The three meandered up the estuary, weaving in and out of the kelp and trying to keep themselves as close to the sea bed as possible. They swam about half a mile up the estuary until the water was too shallow to swim in; very soon they would be crawling in a very shallow river.

"Dad, what's a salt marsh?" said Dylan.

Still snaking in the water, the Captain replied, "It's a coastal area that lies between land and open salt water. It's a place that gets regularly flooded by the tides and there should be lots of places we can hide until dusk."

Dylan nodded.

"Right, I think this is far enough," said Culbert. "Get ready to walk onto the shore, boys." He gestured for the boys to pass him and make their way onto the shore. "Be sure to take in some deep breaths as you come up. You might be unsteady on the sand at first because you've never experienced walking on the land before. But you'll get used to it."

Dylan nodded again, but Axneus showed no sign that he'd been listening at all as both boys started to surface. Dylan was the first to walk out of the sea. He heard a popping noise as his bubble burst around him, covering him in a very fine rainbow mist. He drew a huge breath and started to cough ... another large breath, this one was a little easier ... Coughing and spluttering, he began to walk cautiously from the break. His feet felt too heavy as they pushed down through the thin air, and he kept slamming them into the ground, jarring his knees. Every part of him seemed to be moving much too quickly.

Axneus, however, bounded out of the water, taking no

notice of the advice he had just been given. His bubble popped and he immediately tried to run up the beach to beat his older brother.

Wheezing and spluttering, he fell face-first into the sand after a couple of strides as his knees gave way. He rolled around on the shore, arms shooting up into the air, trying to clamber to his feet.

Now acclimatised, Dylan walked over and held out his hand to help his brother up. "Why didn't you listen to Dad?"

Still panting, Axneus just shrugged his shoulders and brushed himself off, determined to master walking on the land.

Last to appear was Culbert. They heard his bubble pop and watched as he took in some very deep and welcome breaths of the Malotan air.

"Ahh, boys ... I've waited ten years to breathe this air again! Can't you smell it?"

"I can smell something. It stinks," replied Axneus, now almost used to walking on the sand and stumbling only every fourth or fifth step.

"Smell what, Dad?" said Dylan.

The Captain leaned over them and sniffed in another gigantic measure of air, his eyes sparkling. "ADVENTURE!!"

The boys jumped out of their skin. Once they'd got over their fright, they burst out laughing and ran around the beach, screaming and shouting, "ADVENTURE!"

"Boys, please remember we're trying not to draw attention to ourselves. Now, we need to find somewhere to camp out until sunset – then we can go and see Rusty for some homemade stew and fire water!"

He took his bag off his shoulder and placed it in front of the boys, put his hand in his pocket and took out his nose warmer. He lit it and popped it in his mouth.

He took a number of drags on the pipe, then continued.

"I'm going to head off into the bush and get some branches and leaves to make a shelter. I won't be too long – now, I want you two to keep a low profile, and no fighting! Like I said – we can't be seen by the locals!"

"Yes, Dad" said the boys in unison, and sat down by their dad's bag as the Captain reached into it and pulled out a machete. The boys' mouths opened wide at the sight of this monstrous knife.

He winked and said, "Don't tell your mother," and fixed it to his belt. Then he walked off the beach and headed into the bush for provisions.

The Captain walked on through the bush, looking to find some strong bamboo and palm trees to make a shelter. All was quiet, but he had the strangest feeling that he was being watched. He turned to look in both directions, but he couldn't see anything alarming. He continued his search for shelter, swishing his machete from time to time to clear a path.

SWISH ... THWACK ... CRUNCH ... THWACK ... CRACK ... CRUNCH. The Captain was making short work of finding bamboo as he sliced through another shoot and watched it tumble to the floor.

Drawing on his pipe, he picked up the shoot and put it into the bundle that he had already collected, secured with a strong vine.

"Right, that's enough bamboo. Now on to find some palms," he said to himself.

Before he had a chance to move, he heard a twig snap somewhere behind him. He turned quickly, machete wielded ready, to scare who or whatever away, but again, there seemed to be nothing.

Scouting the immediate perimeter, he tried to focus on anything moving. He slowly turned a full circle. Nothing ...

Taking a couple more puffs on his nose warmer, he slowly put his machete back in its sheath and picked up the bundle of bamboo canes. He carried on deeper into the bush, his heart pounding a little.

Back on the beach, the sun beat down on the boys, drying their clothes as they lay back on their elbows, eyes closed, recovering from their most unusual taxi ride.

Axneus opened one eye and whispered, "Dylan? Dylan? Are you awake?"

Dylan's mouth was open, but his eyes were tightly shut. There was no reply.

Axneus didn't hesitate. He took his chance to steal Dylan's forest samphire. Flipping over onto to his knees, he opened Dylan's satchel and began to rifle through it.

Thumbing through notebooks and maps of Maloto as he went, he fumbled around, trying to find the samphire. His hand ran across something wet and slimy. This must be it.

He pulled his hand out of the satchel and yes, just as he thought, it *was* the samphire.

Quickly he closed the bag and laid it back on his brother's chest. Dylan snorted, stirring from his slumber as he did so. Axneus stopped in his tracks, petrified he was about to be caught red-handed.

But Dylan continued to sleep. Axneus blew a silent sigh of relief and sat back, stuffing the samphire into his own bag before lying down on his back, closing his eyes, and pretending to be asleep.

A small lizard ran over Dylan's leg and he woke with a start. "Ax! Was that you? Pack it in!"

Pretending to wake up, Axneus mumbled, "Wh ... what? What do you want, Dylan? I was asleep." He followed this with a dramatic yawn.

"No. Something just touched me. If it wasn't you − then what was it?"

Dylan looked down and saw the little brown lizard staring directly back at him. "Oh, cool! Stay still, little one − I gotta draw you!"

He sat up and reached into his bag, looking for his drawing pad and pencils. It frustrated Axneus greatly that Dylan could draw pretty much anything in great detail with little to no apparent effort. Axneus held his breath, waiting for Dylan to notice that his samphire had been taken. But Dylan was too interested in sketching the lizard.

Dylan pulled out his pad and pencil and began to draw.

"Oh, you're not drawing again, are you?" snapped Axneus, "you're so boring!" Another fake yawn escaped.

"Shh, Ax! You'll scare him away!"

Taking this as an invitation, Axneus stood up and started waving his hands, stamping his feet and making monster noises.

Before Dylan could start drawing, the lizard had scuttled away.

"Axneus, you idiot!" shouted Dylan. "What did you do that for?!"

Axneus shrugged, stuck out his tongue at his brother, and sat down on the sand. This was a well-trodden path for the brothers and usually signalled that a physical altercation was imminent. But just before things boiled over into a full-blown skirmish, the boys heard a call from behind them.

"BOYS! Boys, give me a hand, would you?"

The Captain's timely emergence from the bush inadvertently diffused a full-blown punch-up between the brothers as they both leapt up to help him with his bundle of vegetation.

Culbert thwacked his machete into a piece of rotten driftwood and the three carried the bundle of branches and palm leaves down to the salt marshes, ready to set up their camp.

The Captain cut the vine that held the bundle together and started to jam the thick bamboo canes into the wet sand against the windward side of the salt marsh.

As quick as a flash, he then began to build a makeshift wall and roof by weaving smaller, bendier strips of bamboo in and out to make the wall thick enough to keep out the wind.

"There you go, boys."

The pair looked at him in amazement.

Culbert grinned, proud that he had not forgotten his long-neglected skill. "Some much-needed shade for us, I think. It will keep us cool until we can visit Rusty at sunset." He was well aware that the boys had been about to burst into a fight, but now they both sat under the shelter and searched through their satchels for their lunch.

Tempers cooled along with the sea air as the three sat and talked about their forthcoming adventures. The sun was beginning to set on the island of Maloto, and the pale blue sky was becoming a deep red. There was something a little sinister about it, almost as though it was bringing sadness.

Constantly watching the horizon, waiting for the right time to go in search of Neptune's Tower, the Captain pulled out of his pocket a small hexagonal ivory box with brass fastenings. It was covered with scratches, dents and deep gouges.

He opened up the lid carefully, revealing a battered old tin disc suspended on a pin. The disc was spinning wildly, and on it was painted a thin golden line.

The Captain sat and watched intently as the disc continued to spin.

"What's that, Dad?" said Dylan, shuffling closer on his bottom for a better look.

"This is a special compass that will help us find Neptune's Tower and Rusty. As soon as the sun sets it will point us to exactly where the tower is."

Axneus tried to look uninterested in the compass as he watched from a distance, but the disc continued to spin hypnotically, and even he was mesmerised.

The Captain looked to the horizon and said abruptly, "Right, get your kits together, boys – it's nearly show time!"

The boys reacted to the assertiveness in their father's voice and leapt up, hurrying to pull together their bags ready for the off.

The compass was spinning furiously ... then all of a sudden came to a juddering stop, pointing behind them into the lush green Fijian bush.

"Here we go, boys! This way!" He made sure they had picked everything up and hurried them into the bush.

With the Captain in the lead following the golden pinpoint of the compass, the three walked eagerly through the leaves. "Keep close, boys, I don't want to end up losing one of you. Your mother would never forgive me!"

The Captain was well aware that something was watching them from afar. He upped his pace and made sure the boys were close on his heels. Keeping his mind off it, he began to sing ...

"Farewell and adieu to you, Spanish ladies, Farewell and adieu to you, ladies of Spain, for we have received orders for sail to old England ..." The singing turned into a whistle as he yomped through the bush.

The compass changed direction and so too did the boys; deeper into the bush they wandered.

"I thought you said it was on the beach?" said Axneus.

"No, it moves, Ax – it appears at sunset and disappears at midnight. It's always somewhere on the island, but never in the same place. That's why I made this compass!"

"What's it made from, Dad?" asked Dylan.

"The golden paint is from the tower itself. I scratched it

off and mixed it with some lead paint. It works a treat – it's like a magnet to the old girl!"

Dylan nodded, impressed.

Axneus was about to say something disparaging when they saw a blinding golden flash and heard a loud WHOOMPH as the tower plonked itself deep in the Maloto bush, out of nowhere.

"Aha! Thar she blows, boys!" the Captain roared, triumphant. "This way." He put the compass in his pocket and strode toward the heavy studded wooden door.

CHAPTER 14
NEWS OF MARVIN

The two boys gazed in astonishment at the vastness of the tower and craned their necks to see the top as it climbed up into the darkening Fijian sky.

Culbert turned to the boys. "Now, I haven't seen Rusty for a long while and I don't know if he will recognise me after all these years, so just hang back. The old boy can be a bit fiery and he's very protective of his beloved tower!"

The Captain slowly approached the door and turned the handle, trying to be as quiet as he could. But the handle had other ideas, scratching and screeching as he turned it. He felt the other side of the handle stiffen as somebody grabbed it ... and then the door flew open, pulling the Captain inside.

His face bounced into something hairy and tough. It appeared to be a man's chest. Trying to recover his dignity, he pulled himself away from the matted mound of red hair and looked up.

A craggy, reddened face looked down upon him, eyes burning as fiercely as he remembered.

"Can I help you?" boomed Rusty.

Readjusting himself, the Captain gulped and said, "Is that any way to greet an old friend?"

The looming figure stooped sharply to take a closer look. "What do you mean? I ... hang on ... No. It can't be ... Culbert, is that you?"

"Have you missed me, old boy?"

All the menace and hostility had left Rusty's eyes as the realisation began to set in. "Missed you? You pot-bellied, balding, son of a cod kisser! I've only just stopped mourning your infamous death!"

With that, he picked the Captain up, lifted him into the air like an empty barrel, and squeezed him tight.

"You rotten blighter – the whole island has missed you," said Rusty with a quiver in his voice, as he squeezed harder.

"Easy, soft lad, you've got a grip like a boa constrictor!" Culbert gasped.

Rusty loosened his grip, apologised, and looked over the Captain's shoulder. He frowned as his vision focused on the two small shapes just behind the Captain ... and then a grin spread across his whiskery face. "By Blackbeard's ghost! Who are these two little barnacles, then?"

Still getting his breath back, the Captain introduced the boys. "These are my two sons, Dylan and Axneus. Dylan's thirteen and Axneus is ten. We've come to the island for Dylan's birthday, haven't we, son?"

Transfixed, Rusty breezed past Culbert toward the boys. He crouched down to address them and spoke to them in an unusually soft voice. "Not only has my best friend come back from the dead ... he's brought two little sea urchins for my tea!"

Both boys gasped. Simultaneously, Culbert and Rusty let out loud barks of boisterous laughter like a couple of howler monkeys.

Still laughing, Rusty scooped both boys up in his arms and carried them into the tower. "Mmm. These will go lovely with a slab of cheese and a doorstop of bread!"

The boys wrestled to get the coarse prickly beard off their faces.

Rusty held them tight. "Stop wriggling, little ones! You're soon for the pot!"

Rusty laid on a banquet fit for several kings, a few queens, and a couple of princesses. The boys had never seen so much food; creamy mountains of mashed potato with streams of gravy flowing down them, so many different cuts of meat they didn't know what was what – brown meat, pink meat, white meat ... they left the black meat alone. There were so many vegetables that it looked like the table had its own mini rainforest spreading from one side to the other.

Culbert told Rusty of his meeting with Varuna that fateful night and how she had captured him and taken him to the depths of Lapatia. He told him what he had learned about humans damaging the oceans and rivers.

The boys listened in earnest, as the old sea dogs reminisced about their times on the ocean wave.

Rusty took a monstrous swig from his tin tankard. As the foaming white suds soaked into his unkempt fiery beard, he slammed the tankard on the table and picked up a wild boar leg, devouring the meat. As the half-chewed carcass rolled around his mouth like socks in a washing machine, he used the bone to point at the Captain and said, "In all seriousness, dear fellow, your disappearance really had an impact on the island." He dunked the half-eaten leg into a pot of gravy. "Poor Marvin took it very bad – he blamed himself for your little lost at sea episode – so did most of the islanders, in fact."

Morsels of food were flying from his mouth like depressed

lemmings looking to end it all. "I've heard the sea nymph had him captured. Banished, he was, to the other side of the island." He waved the ravaged leg bone to make his point further. "Never seen him again. That bloody puffin of yours is still around, though." He took another glug of fire water.

Culbert sank into his seat. "It's as I feared. Marvin was blamed for something that wasn't his fault. I wanted to go back and tell him, I really did."

"Don't blame yourself, old man. I'm sure that we would all have done exactly the same thing if we were confronted by a buxom sea beauty like Varuna!" laughed Rusty, slapping the thick wooden table.

"Who's Marvin, Dad?" said Dylan.

"An old friend I used to work with on the island years ago. The day your mother whisked me away to Lapatia, I was out helping him to catch plastic. Your mum grabbed me and pulled me under the sea, and he was blamed for my disappearance."

"That's not fair," said Dylan, "it wasn't his fault!"

Axneus piped up, "That's right. Dad was *cod*napped!"

A deep guffaw bellowed from Rusty's chest. Bits of food flew out of his mouth and found their way into his beard, onto the table, and onto Axneus's face.

"Eurgh! That's rotten!" Axneus recoiled in disgust.

This just made matters worse. Rusty tilted his head back and his shoulders started going up and down violently, with more food flying out of his mouth. The effect was like a ginger volcano.

Paying no attention to Axneus, Dylan turned to his father. "So what are you going to do, Dad? Are you going to find Marvin and tell him it wasn't his fault?"

"First thing in the morning, son," said the Captain.

"Great – it sounds like he's had a really rough time."

Shouting over the gurgling growling din of Rusty, Axneus gestured to his dad. "Can we go soon, Dad? I'm bored ... and it's raining food over here!"

The Captain looked across at the time. It was a quarter to midnight. "Yes, Ax, we should. Time is getting on. And I know what happens at midnight!"

Rusty overheard this and calmed down somewhat. He wiped the tears of laughter from his eyes and brushed all the remaining bits of food from his beard. He also looked at the time.

"My word, yes! Time is getting on and we'll be off soon! ERIC!" he boomed, "Time to clear up, boy!"

Culbert turned to Rusty in disbelief. "No ... he can't still be here?"

Rusty merely nodded and pointed to the entrance of the kitchen at the far end of the room. Culbert expected to see a grown man ... but no, the same slim, scrawny, self-righteous little dark-haired ferret of a sulky adolescent appeared.

"Eric, you've hardly changed!"

"Shame I couldn't say the same about you," sniped Eric. "Still making a mess and expecting other people to clear it up, I see."

"Some things just don't change, I guess," sighed Culbert.

"In this case, sadly not," Rusty agreed. "Still can't get rid of him. He hates the job and I'm pretty sure he doesn't like me much either, but still he stays here moaning that it's all beneath him."

"It is!" Eric piped up. "I'm worth so much more than a pot cleaner!"

Rusty waved him away like an unwanted fly.

"Anyway, Captain, it's getting on. It's almost midnight!"

Culbert nodded and Rusty embraced the three in an all-encompassing hug.

"It's so good to have you back, Culbert. Make sure to come back very soon!"

"It's a promise," said Culbert.

He led the two boys out into the cooling, moonlit night air.

CHAPTER 15
A REUNION

As soon as they stepped out into the darkness, the same
feeling seemed to creep up upon him once more: the
feeling that they were being watched.

It soon became apparent that he wasn't the only one
feeling uneasy, as Dylan looked up at him. "Err ... there's
nothing on the island that likes to eat humans, is there, Dad?"

Culbert didn't look down but replied calmly, "No, son, not
for many, many years now – everything that likes eating
people is in the sea." He continued to watch the perimeter.

Dylan tugged on his hand. "But why does it feel like we're
being watched? Are we being hunted?"

Culbert continued to look silently into the darkness,
transfixed by the silhouettes of the palm trees moving in the
wind. He squeezed the boy's hand. Dylan's vision seemed to
have focused on something.

It felt like an eternity, but all of a sudden a shadow
appeared. The shape was small, but stout and strong. It
looked like ...

"By the Holy Coves of Lapatia, Dad! A BEAR!" Dylan
forgot that he was supposed to be quiet.

But before Culbert could answer, the mysterious shape began to move forward toward the boys, with its arms stretched out in front. It was making a hideous groaning noise. Still unsure of what this was, the Captain turned to go back inside Neptune's Tower. He went to bang on the door, but as he raised his arm there was a bolt of light and the tower disappeared with a FIZZ.

Swinging his fist into thin air, Culbert lost his footing, slipped and fell on his bottom with a thud.

Dylan ran to his dad's aid, tugging at his shirt as he tried to help him to his feet. Axneus screamed and ran off into the forest.

The Captain shouted after him, "AXNEUS! Don't run in there! Come back! It's not safe!"

Axneus just kept running like a bolted horse into the thick dark forest.

Dylan tried also to call him back. "AX! Come back!"

By now the moaning, bearlike figure was almost upon them. Culbert frantically grabbed behind him looking for his machete – only to realise it was still stuck in that piece of rotten driftwood.

"Dylan, get behind me. If it attacks – RUN," said the Captain, preparing for the worst.

"I'm not leaving you, Dad!"

Brandishing the pointed end of his nose warmer, Culbert waved it at the beast.

"Bloody leave us alone!" shouted the Captain.

The beast was on them. It seemed a lot shorter than they had first thought, but it was breathing heavily.

It slowly put out its hand toward them.

Dylan screamed.

Culbert held his breath.

The hand came closer. It appeared to be offering to help them up off the thick forest floor.

Confused, Culbert struck out at it with his pipe. "Go on, bugger off and leave us alone. I need to find my son!"

Holding its recently whacked hand, the beast began to speak. "I can help you look for him, seeing as it was me that scared him off."

With that, the beast put both hands to its head and pulled away a thick furry hood.

"Hello, Capt. It's been a long time, no?"

Utterly baffled, Culbert slowly put away his pipe. Still shaking, Dylan helped him to his feet.

"Do I know you?" asked the Captain.

"Know me? KNOW me? I can't believe you've forgotten about me! OK, so I might look a bit different after all these years, and living in the Forest of Shadows hasn't exactly helped, but surely you can remember your old friend?"

"Who is it, Dad?" said Dylan.

The stranger replied, "Maybe this will jog your dad's memory."

He reached into his jacket pocket and pulled out an old windsock. He shot a wink at Culbert.

"Mar ... MARVIN?"

"Yes, old friend. It's me. Good to see you again!"

"Oh, Marvin, I'm so sorry – I heard what happened to you. Rusty said they exiled you to the Forest of Shadows after I disappeared. It wasn't your fault, Marvin."

Culbert fell on Marvin, losing all of his poise and masculinity. He wept uncontrollably on Marvin's shoulder. "I'm so sorry, old friend. I wanted to tell you, I really did."

Dylan had never seen his father like this before. His dad was always a pillar of strength, always knowing what to do. Watching him cry like a baby on this man's shoulder made Dylan start to realise that his herculean father was just as vulnerable as he was.

"Axneus – my boy – he's in the Forest of Shadows alone. We must find him." sniffed Culbert.

Marvin pulled the Captain's snotty face off his shoulder and said, "Capt, it's my fault your boy ran off. I'll help you look for him. You have nothing to fear, I know these woods better than anyone on Maloto. We'll find him, I promise."

CHAPTER 16

IN SEARCH OF AXNEUS

M arvin told the two of the awful ordeal he'd had to endure after Culbert disappeared. He explained that Marilla had the whole island under a spell and had banished him to the Forest of Shadows, never to return.

He told them about the Midnight Marauders, who Culbert was surprised to learn were actually a very kind and peaceful ancient tribe; they had taught Marvin how to adapt and live in his new surroundings, not fearing the shadows but learning how to move within them, becoming the shadows themselves. Hiding ceaselessly from the villagers' judgement.

"Your son, Axneus – has he ever run off before?" said Marvin, when he had finished his tale.

"No, never," replied Culbert, pulling himself together and brushing the remaining dust off his trousers.

Marvin turned to Dylan and asked the same question.

Dylan answered promptly. "Yes, he used to run away like that at home when we used to play Pirates and I'd make him walk the plank, but I always found him hiding in the cupboard. I don't think there are many cupboards around here, though!"

"OK," Marvin replied, "he ran in that direction." He pointed north-west, further into the island. "He'll probably end up in the Mulgar Mountains. There are lots of caves where he can keep warm."

"Well," said Culbert, putting on a brave face, "best we get moving while the trail is still warm. This is becoming quite the adventure, eh, son?" He gently poked Dylan in the ribs then gestured to him to hold his hand.

"You've never mentioned the Mulgar Mountains, Dad – what are they?"

Culbert explained, never taking his eyes off the surroundings in his search for Axneus.

"Well, son, they're a chain of mountains that look like a row of jagged teeth. People say they're long-extinct volcanoes, but I think this is what really happened.

"Thousands of years ago, the waters around Maloto were protected by many sea guardians. The most famous of these was the fearless Dakuwaga. Part octopus, part man, he was courageous and headstrong, the sea god of the Pacific waters. No other reef guardian was a match for his strength."

Dylan listened in awe as his dad continued.

"But word reached him of an even greater god approaching the reef at Maloto island, intent on conquest. This was Kadavu, a fearsome shark sea god.

"Kadavu, arrogant and proud, flew into a rage and came to challenge Dakuwaga, to claim the isle of Maloto for himself.

"Battles between sea guardians were epic and brutal. They were felt all through the Fijian and Samoan islands, and such disturbances created great waves that crushed and sank many ancient islands.

"One of Kadavu's most famous battles was with Lapoto, a part barracuda, part man guardian who proved to be no match for him.

After defeating Lapoto, Kadavu found nothing of interest on the island of Lapatia and sunk it to the sea bed.

"Is that how Lapatia sank, Dad?" asked Dylan.

Culbert smiled and continued with his story.

"Dakuwaga was expecting Kadavu and was guarding the passage onto Maloto at the mouth of the River Chaos, with a little help from his allies. Being an octopus god, he had eight tentacles. He fixed four of them securely to the rocks and held the other four aloft, ready to fight.

"Kadavu soon found that he was no match for the cunning and strength of Dakuwaga and he was being squeezed to death.

"To make sure Kadavu could cause no more destruction, Dakuwaga pulled out the shark god's teeth and stabbed them into the Maloto landscape before banishing him, never to return.

"This angered Kadavu and he promised to seek his vengeance. As the old prophecy goes, When a child of both Lapatian and human kin is born, he will return to claim Maloto for his own once more.

"That was so cool!" said Dylan, completely in awe of the fantastic story but failing to realise its significance.

"My dad told me that when I was thirteen. Just don't tell your brother as I'll tell him when he's thirteen, too."

Dylan nodded.

Marvin spoke. "If I may be so rude as to interrupt this old fairy story ... I also know somebody who might be able to help us find Axneus. She lives at the base of the Mulgar Mountains. An alchemist, mixer of potions, caster of spells and merchant of the weird and wonderful. If she hasn't seen him then she's sure to have something that can find him for us, but I warn you – she's dangerous!"

"That sounds like a plan – let's go!" The Captain set off, leading them toward the treacherous mountains.

CHAPTER 17

AT THE FOOT OF THE
MOUNTAINS OF MULGAR

The Mulgar Mountain range was a rugged and desolate place, the air foul and putrid with sulphurous volcanic gas. Over centuries the rocks had turned a deep purple. The mountain summits were speckled white with snow and ash, making them look like a row of teeth chomping into the midnight sky.

Culbert, Dylan and Marvin worked tirelessly through the thick forest, forcing their way through the tough bush, heading toward the base of the Mulgar Mountains, keen to see the mysterious sorceress.

Culbert turned to Marvin and asked, "So, who's this wizard? I thought I knew everyone on this island!"

"Technically speaking, she's a witch or a sea nymph. And indeed, you did know everyone – but you've been away a long time, my friend. Her name is Marilla. She arrived one night on the island through the sea mist – nobody knows where from, or for what reason. She was the one who banished me to the Forest of Shadows."

Culbert gasped. "You don't have to do this, Marvin. There must be another way?" He patted his old friend on the back.

Marvin shrugged. "No, she will know, and like I said: you've been away for a long time, my friend. The islanders are dangerous and unpredictable." His head bowed, he walked past Culbert and continued to beat a path through the forest.

"Sounds like the island has changed lots since you left, Dad," said Dylan.

"You could be right, son – and not for the better!" replied Culbert.

Marvin gestured for the two to be quiet and pointed to a spot where the bush seemed to be at its thinnest. "Her cave is through there. We must approach with caution."

"Why? Is she dangerous, Marvin?" said Dylan.

"There's something dark about Marilla," said Marvin, dropping to one knee and finding his way through the opening. "Be careful and keep your distance"

Dylan gulped and nodded.

Marvin nodded and put a finger to his lips, gesturing to Dylan to keep quiet. He pulled the shrubbery to one side, revealing the opening to Marilla's bazaar.

The craggy mouth of the cave showed the flickering shadows of somebody moving wildly inside. Marvin ushered the two forward, and he followed.

Standing in the mouth of the cave, the three were overcome with a thousand different smells and colours that filled the air like a thick sea fog.

There was a silhouette of a large cauldron which seemed to be the cause of the odour; the bubbles and spits leaping from it were mirrored on the wall like an elaborate puppet show.

"What do we do now?" said Dylan.

"Best say hello, I guess. After all, we do need her help ..." said Culbert. "Ahem ... I say, AHOY there! Are you open?"

With that, the erratic shadow stopped dead in its tracks. It slowly turned toward the mouth of the cave and approached them. With every step, the shadow on the cave wall grew larger, arching and stooping over the three until it was almost upon them, looming over them like a spindly tree monster.

"You're late." A willowy, raven-haired lady stepped forward. Dressed in a purple cloak, she was covered in jewellery from head to toe, all of it made from old dead coral. She continued in a more friendly tone. "Dylan, Culbert and Marvin, I've been expecting you. I have a brew on the stove if you care for a drop!"

Quite perplexed, the three looked at each other, shrugged and walked through the mouth of the cave.

"The Marvellous Marilla at your service." She bowed and blew a kiss to Dylan.

Dylan felt himself blushing and hid behind his dad.

"What are you doing, soft lad?" said Culbert, pulling him back him to his side. "Mind your manners, and introduce yourself, young man!"

"I'm D-D-Dylan, pleasure meeting with you." He extended his shaking hand toward the witch.

Marilla turned his hand over and slapped a green looking mess into his palm. "Thanks! I've been looking for a place to put this!"

"What is it?"

"I don't know, it was here when I moved in. It's yours now!"

Dylan retracted his hand in disgust, but the thing was still stuck to his palm. He flicked his hand vigorously and threw the green mess across the room. It made a BOINK noise and a soft splat as it hit the wall, then it slid down to the floor and scuttled off into the safety of the shadows.

Marilla turned to Marvin and raised an eyebrow. "Ah, Marvin, yes. We've met before, haven't we?" She pointed at him knowingly.

"You could say that, yes. It was you who banished me to the Forest of Shadows and stopped me from rescuing Culbert," said Marvin, with an unforgiving grimace on his face.

Dylan's clean hand flew to his mouth to stifle a gasp.

Marilla smiled. "Don't pout, Marvin. It all worked out for the best, didn't it?"

Marvin wrinkled his nose as she continued.

"But this little one, I do not know. This little one, I want to learn all about." She circled Dylan as he stood trying to get all the slime off his hand by wiping it on his trousers.

"Yes. This little one is full of wonder and adventure. There are great things to come for this one. One may even dare to call it magic!"

She knelt down and looked Dylan in the eye. Softly she said, "Don't worry, I know where Axneus is. You'll be together soon enough." She shot him a wink as she stood up. "But come, all of you, come and sit down and drink some of my tea, it will make you feel so much better."

Without hesitation they all sat down on the animal-skinned stools around the large cauldron whose suspicious-looking purple contents were still spitting, fizzing and popping.

Dylan was still absolutely flabbergasted by what she had just told him.

Marilla started to dance around the cauldron, waving a large ladle around and using it like a microphone. She began to sing.

"One dark and starlit night no less, three wanderers came in a terrible mess. No reason why the three dropped by, but I saw that they needed assistance ... Don't worry my boys, he's safe and sound, your fourth comrade will soon be found. Don't look sour, he's in the Tower, so drink, at Marilla's insistence!"

"By the beard of Neptune!! In the tower? How on earth do you know that?" said Culbert in astonishment.

"Now, that would be telling, wouldn't it, you beautiful bearded man!" She was still spinning around. "So, what are you going to buy from Marilla's Marvellous Bazaar? I've got haddock pockets, mermaid's tears, yeti crab claws, squid fingers, and a wonderful line in jellyfish fingernails."

"Jellyfish don't have fingernails," said Dylan.

"No, not anymore, I've got them all!" laughed Marilla. "Oh, I also have cod lips!

"Cod lips?" replied Dylan. "You have cod lips?"

"Yes. I blame my mother." Marilla began to laugh hysterically.

"Er, we're not here to buy, I'm afraid," said Marvin, shaking his head.

Still laughing, and spinning and swirling uncontrollably, Marilla replied, "Ha ha ha! That's a real shame ... The last person who didn't buy anything from me is over there." She stopped laughing abruptly and pointed her dripping ladle to a wooden shelf in the very back corner of the cave.

Dylan wandered over to the rickety shelf and focused on the little glass jar at its far end. He couldn't quite make out what was in there ... then it dawned on him. A tiny little man was waving at him frantically, pleading with him to set him free.

Dylan gasped, stepped back and looked at Marilla in horror. She had stopped spinning now and was looking a little more sinister.

"So, boys, what's it's gonna be?"

Dylan ran over to his dad and whispered what he had just seen on the shelf.

Culbert's eyes turned as wide as saucers. "On second thoughts, we're all really parched, we couldn't buy three cups of that delicious-smelling tea, could we?"

"Five gold coins for the tea. Each," snapped Marilla as she snatched the coins out of Culbert's sweaty palm and shoved them in her cloak pocket.

She spun around and grabbed three crudely hollowed-out coconuts, submerged them in the bubbling brew and tossed one tea-filled coconut cup in front of each of them.

Culbert tentatively picked up his cup and supped on the fizzing and popping suds. He gestured to Dylan to drink.

Dylan's mind jumped straight back to the image of the little man in the jar and he started to quaff the brew. After a couple of mouthfuls, he said, "Are you a siren, Marilla?"

Marvin and Culbert spat their drinks across the fire, giving the illusion of a brief snow shower in the cave.

Marilla stared, serpent-like, at Dylan. "A siren? Young man, do you know what a siren is?"

Instantly wishing he hadn't said anything, Dylan slowly shook his head. Culbert and Marvin were both frozen in fear by Marilla's response.

"Sirens are ancient sea nymphs – flirty, mischievous and dangerous. They lure sailors to their doom with their beauty and melodic songs ..."

The trio started to become drowsy and their vision became blurry and fuzzy. All tried to fight the urge to rest, but it was too strong.

"That's right, my three boys, rest up – all will become clear upon your waking," whispered Marilla.

CHAPTER 18

THE TRIDENT OF FIRE

Dylan's eyes slowly opened. His head felt heavy and dazed. He was still in the cave, but the air was full of a sea mist. He had no idea how long he'd slept. He looked for Marvin and his dad ... but they were nowhere to be seen.

There was no sign of the lit fire or the bubbling cauldron.

There was no sign of Marilla.

"H ... H ... Hello?" Dylan whispered into the mist. "Dad? Marvin? Marilla? Are you there? I can't see anything through this mist. Say something, anybody!"

The room started to fill with a darkness.

A shadow approached.

"Dad? Is that you?"

But the shadow grew larger and larger. It grew to fill the cave. Dylan could make out a shape. It was a man, but his skin was smooth and his head seemed to have sunk into his shoulders. He had a pointed snout. Dylan worked it out with a gasp as the creature moved closer ...

Kadavu.

He was holding a nine-foot trident with glowing red barbed tips.

Dylan screamed at the shadowy monster, "What do you want? What have you done with my dad? Have you hurt them?"

Kadavu said nothing but slowly pointed his trident toward Dylan, its searing hot tips getting closer to the skin on his arm.

"Leave me alone!" bellowed Dylan.

Kadavu lifted the trident and brought it down onto Dylan's arm. Dylan let out a blood-curdling yell. The pain was unbearable. He closed his eyes, turned his head and pulled his arm away.

He felt a second hand grab him on the shoulder. With every ounce of his strength, he screamed and knocked the hand off.

"Go away! Where are they?"

"Dylan? Dylan, are you OK? It's me. Dad."

Dylan opened his eyes and there they were – Marvin and his dad. The cave was exactly the same as before, apart from Marilla who had long since vanished.

"Are you OK, son? Marilla tricked us all. She gave us some potion to send us all to sleep."

"Yes, she swiped all of our money too," said Marvin. Scratching his head in bemusement, he handed a piece of paper to Culbert. "She left a note."

Culbert opened it and read it aloud. "It says, *'sorry about the sleeping potion trick boys, trade's been down recently and a girl's gotta pay for her razor clams somehow! It's true about Axneus, he's in Neptune's Tower with Rusty. Best go and get him at sundown!' Ciao for now!'*"

Glancing out into the beaming sunshine, Culbert said, "Right, well it's morning. The tower isn't due to turn up until dusk, so there's only one thing for it.

"Think it's time we headed back to the old lighthouse – see if we can find ourselves some provisions, get some rest before we get your brother and head home to Lapatia."

Dylan gave his dad a big hug, relieved that the horrible ordeal was just a nightmare. "Great idea, Dad. This place is starting to scare me!"

"Yes, your birthday has been quite an adventure, eh?" Culbert laughed.

Dylan clung tightly around his dad's neck and his mind darted back to his dream. Feeling a sudden sharp pain, he pulled back his shirt sleeve and looked at his arm. There was a fresh burn mark from Kadavu's trident.

He covered it over quickly before his dad could see.

CHAPTER 19

A CLEVER BIT OF KIT (AND ADRIAN AGAIN)

E xhausted, Dylan lay sound asleep on his dad's back. Culbert and Marvin were fast approaching a well-trodden opening, far away from the mangroves and the dense forest, heading back to Bottle Neck Bay and the old lighthouse.

The morning air felt lighter and cleaner than in the thick jungle, and the volcanic stench of the Mulgar Mountains had all but disappeared. Their spirits begin to lift as they saw the bustling market and Dolphin Bay in the distance.

Culbert fumbled in his pocket, looking for his watch. Flipping it out and glancing at it, he said, "It's coming up to eight-thirty. Everybody will be heading to the market, so now would be a good time to head to the lighthouse without being spotted. You're exiled, and I'm supposed to be dead ... so keeping a low profile would be the order of the day, don't you think?"

"Agreed," replied Marvin.

"The lighthouse is that way. We know where Axneus is now, so we can get some shuteye and be ready to pick him up at the tower at dusk. Some of my old stuff might still be at the lighthouse. I need to get a message to Varuna to tell her that we're all safe – she'll be worrying, I'm sure."

"Fine by me, Capt."

They continued to walk over the sand dunes in the direction of Bottle Neck Bay.

"If I can find the Nereus Shell, I can send a message back to Varuna via an old friend," said Culbert, formulating his plan of action. "And I wonder if SID is still operational?"

"SID?" said Marvin. "Who's SID?"

"Sorry. Satellite Intelligence Device – SID for short. It's a very clever bit of kit. SID helped me navigate the most dangerous of oceans single-handedly. She's very clever, too, has a memory of over a million different types of fish in her databank."

"Impressive!" said Marvin. "What about mythical creatures and sea serpents? Does it have those stored in its memory bank too?"

"Why? What do you mean?" replied Culbert.

Marvin looked up to the sky, squinting as a passing seagull drifted past on a warm thermal. "I mean – does it know about folklore, stories of old and ancient myths? Because if it does, then I would suggest you ask it how to defeat a twenty-foot warrior shark god."

Culbert stopped in his tracks and turned around to face Marvin.

"What on earth are you talking about? We both know that Kadavu is an old Malotan story that fishermen and sailors tell their sons to scare them into bed."

"Then why is your son marked with his trident?" Marvin pulled back Dylan's sleeve to reveal the scorched black mark on his arm.

"Wh ... what is that? It looks like ... But still. It could be anything," said Culbert. "A bit of charcoal from the fire at

Marilla's. Or a bit of seaweed stuck to his skin. Probably just needs a wash."

"Don't be a fool, Culbert. Look closer." Marvin tilted Dylan's limp arm so his friend could see the mark in the morning sun.

There it was, clear as day. The black burnt triangular mark of a trident's tip on his arm. Culbert rubbed at it, but it didn't move.

"But they were just stories, Marvin, stuff we used to scare children around the fire. 'If you don't behave then Kadavu will come and gobble you up for his tea!'" Culbert wagged his finger at an imaginary child.

Marvin looked unconvinced. "Well, all I'm saying is that if the ancient stories are true, then your boy has been marked by Kadavu's trident, and he's set to be sacrificed so that Kadavu can be reborn and take what he believes is his. Maloto."

Culbert's face lost all of its hopeful cheer and became stern. He turned and quickened his pace.

"I never should have come back. Quickly, Marvin. We have no time to lose."

As they approached the lighthouse, it looked tired and in great need of some tender loving care. The red and white stripes looked faint and neglected, and the light itself had long since gone out. It was now held in place only by rust.

The pair hunched over and kept their heads low as they approached it. The garden was completely overgrown and unkempt. Culbert shook his head sadly. The garden had once been his pride and joy.

He came to the old gate and pushed his leg against the rotting wood. It started to swing open but then came free from its hinges and fell flat into the overgrown grass.

"Come on, Marvin." He hurried Marvin past the gate and

checked whether anyone could have seen them enter the garden.

"Coast is clear. Look under the rock by the door, my spare key should be there."

Marvin, imitating a crab, moved stealthily toward the front door. He saw the rock and kicked it over. There was a tinkling sound as the key fell from a crevice in the rock.

Marvin bent down and picked it up. "Got it."

"Good man!" Culbert, still bent over with Dylan on his back, walked over like a tortoise and joined him at the front door. "Let's get inside and relax for a bit."

Marvin looked around, then proceeded to open the door. The key met the rusty lock with a squeak, then a screech.

"QUIETLY!" hushed Culbert.

Marvin nodded. He turned the key further, causing a volley of clunks and clicks. "One more turn should do it!" CLUNK, CLUNK. "That's it." He turned the handle and pushed the door open slowly.

They tiptoed inside.

The room lay victim to ten years of neglect. The dust was dancing in the morning sunlight like a swarm of sea nymphs. Marvin grabbed Culbert's arm and guided him inside, shutting the door quickly behind them.

There was a tear in Culbert's eye as he surveyed his former home. He sniffed. "I'm sorry, Marvin old friend. It's just been such a long time since—"

"BRAWK! BRAWK! ENJOY YOUR TRIP! SACK THE JUGGLER!"

Culbert forgot about being sentimental. "Adrian! The little blighter's still alive! Where is he?" he whispered.

Marvin hastily scouted the room but he couldn't see the parrot anywhere.

"Check the rafters." Culbert looked up at the dilapidated roof.

There he was, waddling up and down the rafters. "BUR-GLARS, BRAWK, I'M BEING INVADED! POLICE! COASTGUARD!"

Culbert put Dylan, still sleeping, on the sofa and gestured to Marvin to grab Adrian.

Marvin held his arms out ready to clamp the bird tight. Anticipating his weathered clutches, Adrian shuffled to the other side of the beam, hopping and squawking as he did so.

"That rotten bird," fumed Culbert. He looked around quickly for something to throw. He picked up a dirty pair of ten-year-old socks. The smell was nearly enough to knock him out.

"Phew, these stink!" Without thinking twice, Culbert flung the pair of tightly compressed socks across the room – straight into Adrian's open beak. This was quickly followed by an explosion of bright green feathers that began to drift to the floor.

"Mmpphh," said Adrian.

"Grab him now! Chuck him in his old cage!" shouted Culbert.

"Righto." Marvin seized on the scraggly feather duster and clamped onto him tight. "Got the little fleabag!"

Culbert rummaged in a corner and unearthed an old bent and battered cage. "Quickly, in here!"

Marvin ran across the room and stuffed Adrian into the small opening before slamming the door tight.

"Right. Throw something over the top of him, he'll think it's night time!"

"Mmpphh ... BRAWK! MMMPPPHHH!" resisted Adrian.

Like a magician, Culbert whipped a dirty old dishcloth off the coffee table and laid it on the top of the cage.

All of a sudden, the kerfuffle stopped and there was silence.

"That's done it," whispered Culbert. With that, he placed the covered cage on the table and sat down gently on the sofa where Dylan lay asleep.

Culbert slumped down and rubbed his tired eyes.

The commotion had stirred Dylan. "Dad, is that you?"

"Yes, son. I was just reacquainting myself with an old friend," grumbled Culbert. He reached into his pocket for his nose warmer and pointed to the battered birdcage.

"Where are we?" said Dylan, looking around the front room.

"This is where I used to live. You're inside the light-house," said Culbert distantly, drawing on his pipe. "Now, where did I put it?" he mumbled to himself.

"Put what?" asked Dylan.

"The Nereus Shell. It's an ancient shell that can call specific sea creatures nearby for help. If I can find it, then I can use it to call for Dusty to get a message to your mother."

"It's really messy in here, Dad. What happened?"

"I can explain that part," said Marvin. "After your untimely departure, the villagers broke in to search for clues to your disappearance. No stone – or cupboard, to be more specific – was left unchecked. They turned the place upside down but they couldn't find anything to tell them why you disappeared."

"So, the shell and SID could be anywhere – even stolen – and we have only hours before Neptune's Tower returns and no way of getting home." Culbert sighed. "Come on, think, man. THINK!"

Dylan pointed to Adrian. "Why don't we ask him? He might know where they are."

"Anything's worth a shot, son. Even that." Culbert struck a match on the coffee table leg and lit his pipe, drawing a couple of times then letting out a huge puff of smoke that filled the room.

He walked over to the beaten old cage and rested his hand on the top of the cloth, ready to whip it off.

"Dylan, I want you to ask Adrian where he thinks the shell might be. We don't exactly see eye to eye."

Dylan nodded and came closer, ready to interrogate the bird.

"Now!" Culbert pulled the cloth off the cage and Adrian let out a screech.

Dylan leaned in close to the cage, trying to look friendly. "Hello, you must be Adrian. I've heard a lot about you."

"BRAWK, WHO TURNED ON THE LIGHTS? BRAWK, WHO ARE YOU?"

"I'm Dylan, and I need your help."

"BRAWK, MY HELP? MAGIC WORD, MAGIC WORD?"

"Please," said Dylan, sighing.

"BRAWK. BETTER. WHAT DO YOU WANT?"

"We need to know where the Nereus Shell is. And SID. Do you have any idea where they might be?"

"BRAWK, SOMEWHERE IN THE MESS! VILLAGERS CAME! RANSACK! BRAWK!"

Culbert rolled his eyes. "Knew this would be a waste of time."

"Let me try again," said Dylan. "You like herring, don't you, Adrian?"

Adrian's tone changed. "Yes."

"Well, if you tell me where both those things are, I'll give you as many herrings as you can eat."

Adrian replied, quick as a flash, "The shell is under the old newspapers by the fire and SID is down in the cellar."

"Thank you, Adrian."

Culbert put the dishcloth back over the cage and looked at Dylan in amazement. "Well done, son! We'll be able to get a message to your mother now! Right, Marvin – you go and fetch SID, I'll look for the shell."

"Righto," said Marvin, and scooted off in the direction of the basement.

Culbert put the cloth back on top of the cage and walked toward the large pile of old newspapers alongside the fireplace. He flipped them over and, just as Adrian had said, there was the shell. "Gotcha!" he said. "Adrian. for once you've come in useful."

"How does it work, Dad?" Dylan gazed at the beautiful multicoloured shell.

"This shell used to belong to the mythical yeti crab. You can use it to contact sea creatures. When you've sent the message, the shell turns green. When the message has been received, it turns blue. Look, I'll show you."

Culbert rubbed the dust off the shell. He put it to his mouth and whispered a name into it, before blowing across a hole in its side. A faint quivering whistle resonated around the lighthouse. Culbert kept blowing until his cheeks turned a dark shade of crimson. The shell turned green, then blue.

"Good, the message got to him. Now we wait."

CHAPTER 20
ERIC

The heavy studded door slammed shut as Axneus fell through it onto the cold terracotta-tiled floor of Neptune's Tower. It was empty inside, apart from the warm blaze of the fire and a few chairs.

Eric's spindly frame appeared in the doorway and approached Axneus as he lay heaped on the floor.

"Who goes there?" barked Eric. He picked up the mop, ready to defend himself from the attacking intruder.

"It's me Axneus Culbert McFinn's son we were being chased by a bear and I ran away and I found the tower and I forced my way in I'm sorry."

"Well, Axneus, son of Culbert McFinn, did your father ever tell you it's against the law to break and enter? Penalty for that is being skinned alive, then fed your own skin! Anyway, there are no bears in Maloto. Whatever it was, I hope it gobbled your father up in one bite! That's if you're even telling the truth, which I very much doubt."

"No!" cried Axneus. Still crumpled on the floor, he started to weep uncontrollably into the crook of his arm.

Eric laughed. Compassion had never been his strong

point. "Yes, I'm sure whatever it was has picked your daddy's bones clean and used your brother's carcass as a toothpick," he sneered, miming using the end of the mop handle as a large toothpick.

It was wasted on Axneus, who didn't even look up, but continued to cry in a heap. Eric started to feel bad and sat down in one of the dark brown leather armchairs. He realised that he might have pushed things too far.

"I was only joking," he said, as he used the mop to prod Axneus in a feeble attempt at reassurance. "I'm sure they're fine. There's nothing of a bear's size that lives on land on Maloto – much bigger nasties in the sea, of course, if they were at sea I'd say they were goners – but the land, nah. They'll be fine."

Axneus finally looked up, his eyes red.

"Come on, get up, dry those eyes and sit up here with me. Who needs family? Look at me!" Eric slapped himself on his feeble pigeon chest.

Axneus pushed himself up, used his sleeve as a tissue and sat down on one of the old armchairs by the fire.

Eric continued, "Yes, my dad left me here years ago, and I turned out alright – who needs family, all you need is a big pot of gold and jewels, can't buy nice things with family."

Axneus sniffed and nodded. "I ... I guess so," he said, rubbing his eyes. "But where ...?"

Eric pointed the tip of the mop at him. "Legend has it that the Maloto sea bed is covered in jewels and riches as far as the eye can see, but it's guarded by a sea serpent – a forty-foot monster who patrols the waters at night, protecting his treasure. He attacks and eats anyone who tries to take it. They say his scales are as thick as roof tiles and his teeth as sharp as Maloto fighting daggers.

"That's what I'm interested in, Axneus. I'm saving up all my wages to be able to afford a boat, then I'm going to tell that lump Rusty to stick his job. Then I'm going to plunder all that gold!" Eric rubbed his hands together.

"What about the serpent?" asked Axneus.

"I was hoping you'd ask that! I have an ancient stone that, when in contact with sea water, summons up the serpent. When he arrives, I'm going to take that trident above the bar over there and thwart the wretched beast once and for all. Then all the Malotan treasure will be mine!"

Axneus looked over Eric's shoulder and saw an enormous trident hanging above the bar. It was easily twice as long as Eric was tall. "I don't remember that being here earlier. I would have noticed it," he said.

Eric turned to look at it. "What are you talking about? That's been here all the time. Never moves. Like I said, when old gingerbread-beard is asleep I'm pinching it and getting myself a boat!"

He reached into his pocket and pulled out the ancient stone. It was the blackest object Axneus had ever seen, and it seemed to pull on his very soul. It was mesmerising.

Eric held it up in front of his face. "A mysterious woman by the name of Marilla came in here one day, asking after somebody called Kada ... something. I said I'd never heard of him. So she tossed me this stone, said it would come in handy for somebody passing through."

Axneus shrugged but never took his eyes off the stone. It was as though it had him in a trance.

Eric started to notice the unhealthy fixation Axneus had with the stone, so he put it straight back in his pocket and changed the subject. " You know this place is magic, don't you?"

"Magic? How?" said Axneus.

Eric explained. "Legend has it that this tower is one of three, and it's called Neptune's Tower because each tower is actually one of the arms of Neptune's trident. They say you

can be transported from one tower to another if you know
how ... and the main tower leads you right to the lost city of
Atlantis."

"Do you know how to travel to the other towers?" asked
Axneus.

"No. I haven't even been up to the first floor. I'm stuck
down here, as Rusty is the only one who can go through that
door." Eric pointed in the direction of a gloomy-looking
doorway that was pulsing with a dark blue haze.

Eric continued, "Also, when you're inside the tower, time
stands still. So it can feel like days have passed outside, but
inside it only feels like minutes. For instance, if Culbert is
looking for you, it will feel like days, weeks for him but for
you he could come crashing through that door any second!"

Axneus's eyes started to well again as his thoughts went
back to his dad.

Eric huffed and got up out of the chair. "You're such a
baby! You can stay here until your dad shows up – but you'll
have to pull your weight around here." Eric pushed the mop
into Axneus's chest. "You can start by mopping the floor. I'll
go and get the bucket."

Axneus looked down at the mop, but then something
caught his eye on the other chair. It was the stone! It must
have fallen out of Eric's pocket when he got up. Checking
that the coast was clear, Axneus slowly walked over to the
other chair and grabbed the stone for himself. He looked at it
in wonder.

"The Malotan gold is mine!" he whispered.

Eric returned with an old bucket. "Did you say
something?"

Axneus shook his head and clenched his hand around the
stone so tightly his fingers went white. He put both hands
behind his back.

"Right, I want to see my face in this floor when I get

back. I'm going for a snooze, seeing as I finally have a helper!" Eric turned around and walked out of the room.

Watching every move, Axneus opened up his hand and gazed at the darkness of the Serpent Stone. He slipped into his pocket and tapped it for safekeeping.

"I'm going to be rich!" he whispered.

CHAPTER 21
JUST TICKETY-BOO

Culbert hoped that, with Dusty alerted to pass on the message to Varuna, the birthday trip to Maloto was finally back on track. He puffed on his nose warmer as he began to rummage around the front room of the lighthouse, looking for usable objects for their return trip.

Dylan was sitting in front of Adrian's cage, trying to peer in under the cover to see what he was doing.

They heard a muffled "got it!" from Marvin in the cellar. This was followed by lots of faint clanking and banging from beneath them, and shortly after that Marvin appeared from the darkness, holding a metal briefcase.

Culbert looked at Marvin with renewed hope and clenched his fist in triumph. "Yes, that's it! That's SID!" he smiled, and walked over to Dylan to ruffle his thick blond hair. "This will help us get home, lad!"

Marvin walked over to the table, pushed its current contents onto the floor, and plonked the case down on it with a bang. "Here you go," he beamed.

"Careful!" said Culbert. "SID may be very clever, but she's

also very temperamental." He started to unclip the fastenings on the front of the case.

Marvin and Dylan looked on in anticipation as Culbert slowly opened the lid.

There was a tense pause, then Culbert raised his hands and punched the air. "Yes! Not a scratch!" Although extremely dusty, the contents of the case appeared to be untouched. There was a pair of ancient headphones and a homemade-looking metal box, covered in wires and buttons, with three antennae poking from the top.

"Is that SID, Dad?"

"Certainly is, son, and it looks as good as new."

"What's that button do?" asked Dylan. Without thinking, he went to stab his finger onto a big red button.

"NO, Dylan!" screamed Culbert. "That's the button that wipes the memory!" He grabbed the tip of Dylan's finger, stopping him in the nick of time.

"Oww," said Dylan as he pulled his finger away.

"Don't ever press that button, Dylan. It completely wipes SID's memory and all the data I've been storing for decades will disappear."

"Sorry, Dad." Dylan rubbed his sore finger. "I won't do it again." Marvin gave him a reassuring pat on the back.

"Fire him up then, Culbert," said Marvin.

Culbert gently lifted the metal box out of the suitcase, revealing yet more buttons, knobs and levers, of all different shapes, colours and sizes.

He pointed to a small circle of wire mesh in the top right-hand corner. "SID's voice box. Made it all myself."

Culbert ran his hand along the back of the box and found a rocker switch. "Right, fingers crossed," he said as he flicked it to the ON position.

"Don't you need to plug it in or something?" asked Dylan.

"No – it runs on solar and lunar energy. I found it was too

much of a drain on the boat's engine when we were out at sea. It's fitted with small solar panels that give it a charge," replied Culbert as he moved it into the sun.

The sun's glaring rays shone directly through the window onto the solar panels, and immediately there were flickers of life as lights began to flash. There were buzzing and beeping noises.

"IT'S ALIVE!" shouted Dylan in excitement, but this was met very quickly by Culbert putting a finger to his lips.

A groan came from the mini speaker.

"SID? Come in, SID. Are you there?"

"What do you want?" said a woman's voice. She sounded cross.

"Huzzah! It works!"

Marvin and Dylan looked confused. "I thought SID would have a man's voice," said Dylan.

"At first it did, but a bit too much salt water got into the circuitry and ever since then SID has been a girl ... I must say I prefer it!"

"Well, that's probably because women are better than men," said SID.

"OK, SID, that'll do," said Culbert. He looked at Dylan apologetically. "I forgot she can be quite grumpy, especially in the mornings."

"SID, I'm sorry about waking you up – but we need your help," continued Culbert.

"What do you need?" the box replied tinnily.

"We need to get a message to Varuna in Lapatia."

"I see," said SID. "Good morning, SID! How are you, SID? I'm very well, thank you, Culbert. I've been stuck in a briefcase in a cellar for God knows how long, so as you can imagine, I'm just tickety-boo." Culbert rolled his eyes as the voice continued. "I mean, not even a how are you? No, just straight to it! Do this, SID. Find me that, SID."

There was a pause. A solitary red light blinked sulkily.

"OK. You win. Searching Lapatia in database ... processing ... Please wait ... processing ..." SID clunked and clicked and whirred. "Results found: Lapatia. The lost underwater village. Coordinates located and stored, location two miles off the southern coast of Samoa. Sunrise 06:34, chance of rain thirty percent, wind speed is two knots and blowing from a south-easterly direction. Now what?"

"What an amazing piece of machinery," said Marvin in astonishment.

"We're going home!" Culbert said with a sigh of relief as he hugged Dylan. "We just need to find your brother now, and head home."

"Do we have to?" Dylan joked. His face was being squashed by his dad's arm as Culbert hugged him.

"Yes, son. We do. We can't go home without him. SID, save coordinates for Lapatia."

"Coordinates saved. Do you require another location?"

"Why not try to locate Neptune's Tower?" suggested Marvin. "It may not work, I know it's inland and it always lands in a different location – but SID found Lapatia ..."

"Worth a try," said Culbert. He leant forward and asked SID to find Neptune's Tower.

SID promptly started flashing and whirring. "Processing ... processing ... processing" – there was an ominous buzzing noise – "no result found."

"Worth a try," said Culbert, unconcerned. "We'll just have to do it the old-fashioned way." He tapped his trusty compass.

SID interrupted. "Is there anything else you need from me?"

"Not just now, SID. Thank you for your help! Do you think you'll be up for a trip with us?"

"Well it beats being in this mackerel-smelling lighthouse

for the rest of my days and listening to Adrian moaning. Yes. Count me in!"

"Great! Now, I'm going to leave you in the capable hands of my good friend Marvin. He will take you back to the harbour and install you on his boat while I go to find my son.

"Dylan. You and I are going to go and get your brother from Neptune's Tower. It's time we headed home. We've had quite the adventure for your birthday, haven't we?"

"I actually think this is the best birthday present I've ever had!"

Culbert sent Marvin off to get provisions for their journey back to Lapatia, and told him to install SID onto the Flying Fox and synchronise with its current navigation system.

"Got it," said Marvin as he whirred into action. He put SID back in the metal briefcase and tucked her under his arm as he headed for the door.

"Make sure not to be spotted, Marvin. You're still exiled, remember?"

Marvin tutted, sighed, and headed out of the weather-beaten front door with SID as a muffled voice in the corner said, "Brawk, enjoy your trip!"

Flick, slap. Flick, slap. Flick, slap, swoosh, sigh.

Axneus mopped the floor, feeling tired and uninterested in his tedious task. His mind was far away, thinking of all the wonders that lay on the sea bed of Maloto.

He huffed again and stopped mopping. "Eric? Eric? When can I have a rest?" he shouted into the next room.

"When I say so," came the muffled response.

Axneus decided to ignore this instruction. He sighed and flumped down in the old leather armchair. Unknown to him, he'd picked his dad's favourite place to sit in Neptune's Tower.

He rested the mop handle on the table and ventured into his pocket to inspect the Serpent Stone once more.

The stone was completely smooth and black, like onyx. It felt heavy to hold, as though it had something denser inside it. Staring at the stone, Axneus's mind moved into a deep black void of the nightmare realm.

He held it up to eye height. It drew his gaze deeper into itself.

This time the dark void seemed to be moving and swirling.

Flashes of burning amber fire started to appear in the heart of the stone, and began to form themselves into a shape.

Curious, Axneus looked deeper into the stone, trying to work out what the shape was. It was trying to manifest into something, but he couldn't quite see it yet.

Then it became clear. The warm amber flames turned a cold yellow, with an even deeper black chasm at their centre. Axneus realised he was looking at the piercing eye of a reptile.

He heard a whisper that seemed to drift into his mind like smoke. "Axneus ... Axneus, there is a great darkness in you. Release me from this cursed place and set me free. I will reward you greatly – I know you covet my treasure, Axneus ..."

He dropped the stone on the hard floor with a clatter.

Recovering himself, Axneus looked up and called out to Eric, "Did you say something?"

"No, you little shrimp, although I was about to ask what the clattering noise was. But what I can't hear is you mopping. What are you doing in there?"

Eric's threatening tone snapped Axneus out of his trance. The eye disappeared and the stone returned to its original colour. He picked it up with his fingertips and put it back in his pocket.

"S ... Sorry, Eric, sir – I was just refilling the bucket with clean water." He lifted himself out of the chair, grabbed the mop and scuttled over to the place where he had left off.

"Sir ... I like that!" replied Eric. "I like your attitude, shrimp. Keep it up!"

Axneus went back to mopping the floor, but his thoughts were firmly fixed on that eye and the message he'd heard.

Perhaps he'd nodded off in the chair and dreamt the whole thing, but he didn't think so ...

Jamming the mop head in the dull water, he swished it around and slapped it back onto the orange tiles. BANG.

That was a bit odd, he thought. Mops didn't usually go bang.

He tried again.

BANG.

"Keep it down in there! You break that mop and I'll break you!"

Axneus poked his tongue out in the direction of Eric's voice. He picked up the mop and tried it one more time. He dunked the head into the bucket, pulled it out like a washed cabbage, and plonked it on the floor. Slap.

Axneus rolled his eyes. What an idiot, he thought. Maybe I just need a rest. He stopped and rubbed his eyes.

He pulled the stone out from his pocket. It was still dark and showing no sign of movement. Just a smooth, shiny stone.

He heard it again.

BANG. BANG. BANG.

"Shh ... Keep it down in there, shrimp. If you wake up that red-headed lump, we'll all be for it. If I hear one more bang I'm coming in there, OK?"

No sooner had the threat had left Eric's lips than ...

BANGBANGBANG.

"Right that's it, you little sea slug! You're for it!"

Eric walked through the door, trying his hardest to look tough. His jaw was clenched, he had puffed out his chest and he held his arms out sideways as though he was carrying something under them. He came up to Axneus and kicked over the bucket onto the floor. There was filthy water everywhere.

"I warned you, you little dolt – I'm going to give you such a pasting."

Axneus cowered. He'd never experienced being bullied before, having only ever been the bully in his relationship with Dylan, and he didn't like it one bit.

"Please don't hit me," he whimpered, "it wasn't me! I don't know where those bangs came from!" He covered his face and backed away toward the door.

"I'm going to enjoy this. All those times Culbert embarrassed me here, and now you're here to take his punishment. How kind of you. How dare he treat me like that? Does he not know who I am – or who my father is?" Eric pulled back his arm with venom. His fists clenched and his knuckles went white with fury.

Axneus's back was flat against the door now and tears were streaming down his face. Anticipating Eric's punches, he put his hands up ready to soften the impact.

Eric laughed. "Don't worry about your pretty face, shrimp. I'll go and get the dustpan and you can brush up all your teeth when—"

BANGBANG.

Eric stopped, lowered his fist and looked around the room. "What on Bluebeard's ghost?" He looked at the door. It sounded like it was coming from there.

"Out the way, you little dweeb." He shoved Axneus to the floor, away from the wooden door, and knelt down to look through the keyhole.

He couldn't see anything on the other side. It was just blackness. Then, all of a sudden, the door smashed open, sending him flying across the room.

"WHHAAAAAAA!" screamed Eric as he soared through the air. He looked like a trapeze artist – but unfortunately for him, there was nobody to catch him on his way down.

"NOOOO!" he bellowed, as he noticed that his face was

heading directly for the bucket. He waved his arms in the air, furiously trying to correct his collision course.

It was too late. Eric's head wedged itself tightly into the manky old bucket with a KER-PLUNK.

This cheered Axneus up no end. He let out a tremendous guffaw, followed by side-splitting titters. His tears of fear turned to tears of joy as he watched the bully twisting and squirming, struggling to free himself from his temporary prison.

"Mmpphh. Help me!" mumbled Eric, his hands tugging at the rim of the bucket.

Carried away by this joyous moment, and forgetting that something had just broken in through a very heavy wooden door, Axneus got to his feet and went to grab the mop.

This was a feeling that Axneus knew all too well. He had the opportunity to do the right thing. Even if Eric was being mean to him, this was his chance to help somebody who was in pain. He knew what to do.

He grinned with glee as he unscrewed the head of the mop, ready to start whacking the side of the bucket as hard as he could.

"This is for making me mop the floor!" He tightened his grip and swung with all his might. DONGGG. The sound echoed around the room like a tolling bell.

Axneus laughed with venomous glee and pulled back, readying himself for another swing.

"This is for being rude about my dad." Axneus took another giant swing at the oh-so-easy target. DONGGG.

"Please stop," begged the quiet voice from inside the bucket. "It really hurts!" Eric put his hands on the bucket, trying to stop his ears from ringing.

"And this one" – DONGGG – "is for trusting me!" Axneus's laughter had now turned to spite and his laughing face was painted with a fierce grimace. "I'm going to keep doing this until you pass out or go deaf!"

Axneus pulled the mop handle back above his head with all his might, ready to unleash repeated whacks to the defenceless Eric, who had his hands raised in surrender.

"I'll show you, you creep!" Axneus closed his eyes and brought his hands down from above his head like a rocket.

But they didn't move. Something had grabbed them in mid-flight.

"That's QUITE ENOUGH, Axneus," boomed a very familiar gravelly voice. Axneus opened his eyes.

"Dad!" he shouted, as he let go of the mop handle and turned around to meet the welcome arms of his father.

Culbert crouched down and gave him a big hug. "Now then, what's all this hitting poor Eric on the head about?"

Through tears of joy, Axneus stuttered, "H ... He deserved it, Dad. He was being so horrible to me."

Dylan appeared from behind Culbert. He gave his brother a look of disdain and brushed past, looking to help Eric remove the beaten bucket from his head.

With a reassuring rub on his back, Culbert continued to give little Axneus some sound advice. "Listen, son, just because somebody is horrible to you, doesn't mean you can be horrible straight back.

"The ancient sea gods see all and know all. And the way that you deal with your problems is seen by all the gods – and they will take their vengeance. Deal with your problems with compassion and love, and the gods will look on you favourably. Mirror violence with violence and the gods will only punish you further."

"Whatever, Dad. Have you finished?"

"You're safe now, but you must never run away like that again. What would your mum say if you went missing?"

Axneus's attitude softened. Putting his head in the crook of his dad's arm, he muttered, "Sorry, Dad."

Meanwhile Dylan had both his hands under the lip of the bucket, trying to wrench it off Eric's head.

He put one foot on Eric's groin to get better leverage and started to pull with all his might.

"MMMPPPHHH!" whimpered Eric.

"Nearly got it!" said Dylan cheerfully, "One last pull!"

Dylan felt the bucket loosen and he pulled harder – and the bucket flew off Eric's head with a popping sound.

"Oww! Me ears! They'll be ringing for days now! McFinn, your bloody kids are out of control!"

"You deserved it!" pouted Axneus and stuck out his tongue in Eric's direction.

Eric ignored him and scuttled off into the other room, wanting to be alone to lick his wounds.

"Dylan, come on, lad. We've got your brother – let's go," said Culbert.

Dylan wandered over and joined in the family embrace. "Good to have you back, brother," he said.

Culbert released himself from the hug and shouted out to alert Rusty of their presence – but there was no reply. He tried once more, louder this time. Still nothing.

Culbert shrugged and took the boys' hands as the three walked out of the door.

"I don't know about you two, but I'm ready to go home," said Culbert.

Both boys nodded their heads wearily.

CHAPTER 23

SMUGGLERS' PASSAGE

R eunited, the three stepped victoriously out of Neptune's Tower into the mangroves of Maloto, with a renewed hope of getting home, getting back to Varuna, getting back to normal.

Axneus had dried his tears and the two boys resumed their usual roles, squabbling and fighting each other every time their dad's back was turned.

Culbert was still fully aware that they must keep a low profile. Their voices became hushed as he tried to locate a small walkway running along the cliff side. This path acted as a handy shortcut to the harbour and, more importantly, was hidden from the eyes of the villagers.

He uncovered some ground moss with his foot. "This way, I think, boys." He pointed to the cliffs and to what looked like a vague pathway along them.

"Why are we going this way, Dad? It's the wrong direction!" said Axneus, scowling.

Instantly remembering what a carbuncle on a barnacle Axneus could be, Culbert snapped, "Actually, son, I'm looking for Smugglers' Passage."

"What's that?" asked Dylan.

Freeing the last of the soil and grass at the edge of the cliff with his foot, Culbert unearthed a pathway that hadn't been used for centuries. He saw an opportunity for a story, and began to explain the significance and dark past of the path.

"Centuries ago, Maloto was a regular overnight stop for the Spanish and Dutch merchant galleons that used to deliver rare and exotic cargo, spices, jewels and rare artefacts all around these islands."

Dylan bent down to help his dad free the earth with his foot, revealing more of the path, as Culbert continued.

"But these large galleons couldn't get close enough to the harbour as the coral that surrounds the island is extremely high, beaching any vessels that are too large. Galleons would have to weigh anchor before the Purple Wall and the sailors would row the rest of the way in a smaller boat."

They had cleared the narrow walkway and now they began their descent onto the cliff face.

With a wave Culbert ushered the boys in front of him and continued his story.

"Smugglers and pirates got wise to this arrangement. They would offer a ferry service to the unsuspecting sailors and crew who wanted to get ashore for sleep and food and ... ahem ... female company.

"They would ferry them into the harbour and around Bottle Neck Bay. Most would head into the Dolphin Tavern – whilst the pirates headed back to the ship, ready to plunder all they could!"

"Clever pirates!" remarked Axneus. He put his hands in his pocket and rubbed the onyx stone with the tips of his fingers, thinking about all the treasure that awaited him.

"So why use the passage then, Dad? asked Dylan.

Culbert continued. "Well, they would then make their way back along Smugglers' Passage and off to the safety and seclusion of the Mulgar Mountain caves, to either sell on or divide the plunder among themselves."

"Greedy bloody pirates!" growled Dylan.

Culbert chuckled.

"Less of the language, son! But you'll be pleased to know that most of the 'bloody pirates' fell to their deaths after they lost their footing on the old hand-woven rope bridge between Bottle Neck Bay and Peanut Cove. Many of them came to an untimely end on the jagged rocks below."

Culbert leant in closer to the boys, speaking in a sinister voice.

"Some say that at night, ghostly apparitions of pirates and smugglers walk the passage and patrol the rope bridge looking for their lost doubloons and pieces of silver, chopping down anyone who comes between them and their treasure!"

Axneus looked over the cliff edge and thought, "I must remember this spot when we get back home. Even more gold for me!"

The pathway was uneven and had been crudely carved into the side of the mountain. The cliff face was on their left-hand side; on their right was a sheer drop into the crashing blue waters below.

"You must hold onto my hands here, boys, it's getting very treacherous," said Culbert.

As they rounded a corner, they could see the harbour – and in it, the Flying Fox. There was a blurry blob on the boat that looked like Marvin.

"Great, he's ready ... I think ..." Culbert said, pointing at the little shape in the distance.

"Time to up the pace! Boys, we're heading home!"

The boys' pace quickened as they knew that their adventure on Maloto was coming to a close.

The pathway was getting thinner and more treacherous with every step. In some places it was no more than a footstep wide, with great chunks of earth falling away. Making matters worse, the wind had grown stronger.

"Boys, be careful, the wind is getting up. Don't get blown into the sea!" warned Culbert.

The waves below them boomed louder and louder. Every crash on the rocks sounded like an explosion and sent a wash of sea spray shooting up the side of the cliff face.

"I can see why those pirates fell into the sea, Dad!" shouted Dylan. "This is really dangerous!"

"Don't panic, boys. Just keep calm and focus on your footsteps," said Culbert. "We're nearly at the rope bridge that joins us to Peanut Cove."

Seagulls squealed and screeched overhead as they struggled in the strong sea winds. Grit and rocks were now beginning to break free from the side of the cliff, blowing into the boys' eyes and making it harder to see.

They could now make out the old hand-woven rope bridge, swinging violently in the strong gusts. Some of the wood had rotted away, leaving great gaping holes in the bridge. The remaining parts were wet through and covered in treacherous-looking seaweed.

The bridge appeared to be supported entirely by strong anchors at either end. It looked very loose and tired.

The wind was getting stronger with every minute, almost as if it was trying to stop them from getting across.

"It's getting worse, boys. We must get across this bridge and off the cliff," shouted Culbert over the din. "Dylan, you go first, Axneus next, and I'll follow." He pointed forward across the slippery planks. "Go on, lad. No time to lose."

Dylan took a deep breath, summoning his courage.

He stepped out onto the first wet wooden slat.

He put his foot down tentatively ... the wood took his weight, and he breathed out with a sigh of relief. He could see the next slat was loose and rotten, so he stepped over it and moved securely to the next.

"Good lad!" Culbert bellowed. "Keep going!" He turned to Axneus and motioned him to step forward and follow his brother.

"Axneus, pay attention to the steps your brother is taking. One slip and you're a goner."

Axneus wasn't paying any attention. He was too busy thinking about his soon-to-be fortune. He put his hand in his pocket and rubbed the stone once more, for luck.

"Axneus! Your turn! Steady steps across, look at where your brother is stepping and follow him." Culbert pushed Axneus gently onto the first plank, and then followed.

The wind was cutting in sideways and the three had to lean into it to stay upright. The sea crashed hard into the rocks below. The soaking wet bridge swayed from side to side, making it even harder to cross.

"Boys, quickly, this isn't getting better," said Culbert. Even he was beginning to sound concerned. Dylan was halfway across the bridge now, carefully considering every step.

Axneus was getting impatient. "Hurry up, sponge-for-brains, I'm getting soaked up here!" He was so busy insulting his brother that he didn't notice where he was stepping. One of the slats broke away and his leg fell through the hole.

"AAAAAAAHH! Help!"

Dylan, shocked to hear the scream and the sound of wood cracking, turned around in horror. The bridge wobbled violently.

Culbert shouted, "Don't panic, Axneus, just hold on tight to the rope."

Axneus reached out and got a hold of the wet rope. He started to pull his leg free.

"Dylan, keep going, you're nearly there!" shouted Culbert.

Dylan faced forward again, focused on his steps and continued gingerly on his way.

Axneus had his leg nearly free, but his pocket was caught on a splintered piece of wood. The wind was howling around him, making it hard to keep his balance.

"Just pull your leg free, and get across. You're nearly there!" shouted Culbert from behind him.

Axneus pushed up hard and his leg was free, but the wooden splinter stayed stuck in his pocket. He heard a rip.

The contents of his pocket tumbled into the violent wash below.

He reached down, trying to catch it – but it was too late. He could only watch as the onyx stone he treasured so much plummeted onto the rocks below, forever lost.

He let out a blood-curdling noise. "NOOOO! My treasure!"

"Don't worry about your marbles, Axneus, just get your leg free and get over the bridge before we all follow them!" yelled Culbert.

Dylan was nearly safe. He only had one more slat to step on and he would be on the other side.

He took a deep breath and stood on the last piece of rotting wood. Breathing a sigh of relief as it held, he continued onto the land, safe and sound.

Still distraught, Axneus got to his feet and continued along the rope bridge. Furious, he folded his arms and stomped his way across.

"Axneus! For Bluebeard's sake! Hold on, boy!"

"I don't care if I fall in now," pouted Axneus, completely ignoring his father and the tempest blowing around his ears.

Dylan shouted, "What are you doing, you idiot? It was only a stone." Dylan looked around, saw an equally sized stone and promptly picked it up. "Look, you can have this one!"

"NO! I WANT MY ONYX STONE!" bellowed Axneus back at his brother.

"Now is not the time to have a squabble, you two!" shouted Culbert from behind them as he continued his trepidatious journey over the rope bridge.

The bridge was now swaying like a Newton's cradle in the wind. Culbert, being bigger than the boys, was finding it harder to keep his footing and grip along the slippery, sodden wood.

Axneus stepped nonchalantly off the final slat and sat down on a large rock behind Dylan to continue his sulk.

Dylan watched in disbelief, appalled that his brother wasn't even interested in the welfare of their dad, who was still in grave danger.

Culbert looked down at the frothing, spewing swell below. It seemed so violent, as if something had been unleashed and was thrashing itself free. A wave full of foamy brine hit him hard, causing him to lose his footing and skid on the slippery surface of the bridge.

"DAD!" shouted Dylan, reaching out his hand at the end of the bridge.

"Stay there, Dylan, I've got this under control!" Culbert shouted as he regained his footing and began to creep along the bridge once more.

Another wave of foam and spray smashed into the bridge. Culbert looked like he had been slapped in the face by a squid.

"Phew, that was a big one!" he joked.

"Dad! Just hurry up and get over here!" But as Dylan beckoned his dad to safety, he noticed something over his father's shoulder – a shadowy apparition at the other end of the bridge. It was wearing a tricorn hat and seemed to be brandishing a rusty cutlass.

Another wave crashed into the bridge and obscured his view.

When the spray cleared, the apparition had gone.

Dylan turned to his brother. "Axneus! Did you see that? It looked like a pirate!" Axneus shrugged and continued to scuff the dirt with his toe.

Dylan lost his temper. "How on earth can you still be worried about that bloody stone when Dad's in trouble?"

"You don't understand! That stone was going to make me rich!"

Dylan laughed and punched Axneus in the arm. "Oh, Ax. You and your little boy fantasies. You idiot, we're already rich enough – we have each other. I can't wait to get home and see Mum and be a family again. Anyway, if it wasn't for Dad you'd still be cleaning the floor in Neptune's Tower!" Dylan whacked his brother again, hoping it would punctuate his point.

Axneus rubbed his arm and stared into his brother's eyes.

"Who needs family? That stone would have given me all the treasure in the world."

Dylan was dumbstruck – he had never heard his brother talk of money and possessions so ruthlessly before.

Another crash and an explosion of spray covered Culbert, who was about halfway across the bridge.

Shaking his head in disbelief, Dylan went to focus on his dad again. He saw that, although slow, he was making progress.

Another wave obscured Dylan's view as his dad shouted, "Nearly there, son! Won't be a tick!"

The spray cleared ... and there it was again: a ghoulish apparition at the other end of the rope bridge, wielding the cutlass above its head.

It was hard to get a good look at the figure – the sea spray was making it almost impossible to see – but he looked like his skin was melting and his eyes burned redder than the flaming fins of the legendary hellfish.

"Dad! Quickly! Get to the end!" yelled Dylan as another violent wave hit the bridge.

The ghoulish character started to cut the rope.

"Just a couple more feet!" shouted Dylan, reaching out to help his dad.

As soon as Dylan put out his hand to help his dad to safety, the bridge fell away to one side, the horizontal path becoming nearly vertical. "Wooaahh!" shouted Culbert. He managed to grab hold of the remaining side of the bridge that was still attached to its anchor.

"DAD! Hold on!" bellowed Dylan.

"I'm doing my best, son! This is madness. If I fall – tell your mother I love her!"

These words stirred Dylan's heart. An anger that he couldn't control was building inside him. He felt the rage consuming him. He clenched his fists and fixed his gaze on the fiendish ghoul at the other side of the bridge.

The tighter Dylan's fists clenched, the calmer the sea below became, almost as if the sea was pouring its violence into him. The fury was indescribable and his face became contorted as he watched his dad in peril.

Although completely disinterested in his dad's life-or-death situation, Axneus noticed that the seas below had formed into two swirling balls like his brother's fists. In disbelief he sat up off the rock and looked down.

The ghoul was now hacking its way through the second rope. Snaps and cracks could be heard echoing across the clifftop.

"LEAVE HIM ALONE!" Dylan roared. He instinctively pushed his fists out in front of him ... and, unbelievably, the giant balls of water followed. They rose violently out of the sea and crashed straight into the ghoulish spectre, instantly vaporising it.

The residual wake broke against the cliff face, flowing back to the waters below.

Dylan sank to his knees, exhausted and shaking.

Axneus, feeling awestruck and a little sheepish, walked over to him and said, "How in the name of Neptune's trident did you do that?"

Dylan whispered, "I have no idea. It felt like ... like I was being controlled by the sea itself."

Axneus looked up to see where their father was. There was no sign of him on the broken bridge. "We're too late. Dad's gone."

Panic-stricken, Dylan looked around for his father. He clambered up from his knees and walked over to the side of the cliff where the bridge had been connected.

He let out a sigh of relief as he saw Culbert clinging onto the side of the cliff face beneath him. "Couldn't give me a hand, old chap, could you?" joked Culbert.

Dylan reached down to help his dad get to the edge and to safety. "Axneus, do something useful and help me."

Astonishingly, the sea below was as calm as they had ever seen it, and the tempest had dropped completely.

"Grab his other arm, Ax, and let's haul him up."

With a massive heave, the two brothers pulled their dad up over the edge of the cliff to safety. They all collapsed on their backs, breathing sighs of relief and staring at the clear blue sky.

"Thanks, boys," said Culbert, getting his breath back and sitting up. "How on earth did we all survive that?"

"I have no idea," said Dylan. "Did you see that ghost on the other side of the bridge? He was trying to cut the rope!"

"What ghost?" replied Culbert and Axneus in unison.

"Axneus, you saw it, right? It was awful-looking. A pirate, or something, with dripping white skin and burning red eyes."

"I didn't see anything. I was too busy trying to find a way to help Dad to safety!"

Dylan bit instantly. "You're such a liar, Axneus McFinn! You just sat there moping over that stupid stone."

Culbert smiled to himself at how quickly things could go back to normal after such an enormous drama.

"Boys, boys. Calm down, we're safe now, and that's all that matters. Let's catch our breath and head down to the bay to find Marvin."

CHAPTER 24

THE GOBLET OF THEA

"DAMN."

Marilla took her hands out of the large silver goblet in front of her. The cup had silver-encrusted waves running along its lip. The waters were dark and stormy.

She flicked her hands a few times to dry them, then tentatively turned around to face the looming shadowy creature which sat in the corner of her cave.

The creature growled, "So, did it work? Did the three McFinns perish under the power of the Goblet of Thea?"

Marilla shook her head and went down on one knee, her head bowed. "My lord ... the Goblet of Thea has always dealt accordingly with those whom I cast unto it, but there is a power too great to control in those little ones," she said. "I have never seen anyone wielding such power over the sea. Our plans could unravel if they learn their heritage."

A long, disconcerted silence came from the darkened corner of the cave. After an uncomfortable pause, the sinister shadow responded with a grimace.

"So. It seems we have underestimated this little sea

urchin,I wonder..." pondered the creature, his black, lifeless eyes burning into Marilla.

"My lord?' Marilla looked puzzled.

"Centuries ago I foresaw that a first born of Lapatia & Maloto would return to these islands. It is he who will help regain my power, it's not the Father we seek it's the boy"

Marilla interrupted him.

"One of the brothers is pure of heart and strong of will, that must be him, but the other, I believe, may be corruptible. He could hold the key to bringing the chosen one to you."

"Do what is necessary, Marilla. Be warned, however, that I will not accept failure next time."

The shadowy creature stood up and stooped over Marilla. A waxy grey claw appeared from the shadows, followed by a forearm as thick as a horse's leg.

The claw grabbed Marilla around the neck and lifted her a clear four feet from the floor. The monster stared deep into her eyes.

"I really hope I don't have to adminster the same punishment as I gave your sister. For your sake, you should hope the same."

The beast's hand tightened around her neck and fear rushed across her face as she struggled to breathe.

She managed to speak. "Of course, my lord. You will become whole once more, I assure you, and claim these islands as your own. I will not fail you," she squeaked.

The monster released his grip and Marilla fell in a crumpled heap.

"See that you don't." He returned to the dark shadows of the cave.

Rubbing her throat, trying to soothe the scratches, she added, "I forgot to mention, my lord, that the younger McFinn boy has unleashed one of your deadliest soldiers."

"Interesting. Who?"

"Gata, my lord." Marilla replied. "I gave the stone to the bar hand at Neptune's Tower, and somehow the McFinn boy ended up with it. Gata's corruption has already warped his mind; he can be manipulated."

"Is he free from his onyx stone tomb?"

"Yes, my lord. He was dropped into the waters around Smugglers' Passage."

"Excellent. Gata will not fail me as you have. He is a trusted and loyal soldier. He will claim what is mine and bring the boy to me. Make sure he receives that message."

"Understood, my lord." Marilla bowed toward the unseen figure lurking in the shadows.

CHAPTER 25

A SIGNAL FROM AN OLD FRIEND

D ylan's mind was beginning to wander as the hot Fijian
sun beat down on him. He looked across at his
brother, who was rummaging through rocks and dust, looking
for stones. He turned the other way to see his dad wringing
out his hat and picking bits of seaweed out of his beard.
Dylan smiled to see them both safe.

He turned to look out to sea and a glint of something
caught his eye. He saw a grey object, very small but distinct,
fly up out of the sea and splash down again. Fixing his gaze on
the one spot he saw it again. Up ... and splash.

"Hey, look at that," said Dylan as he pointed out the
unidentified object.

"Son of a cod fish! It's Dusty!" shouted Culbert, who
began waving uncontrollably out to sea.

"Neptune's trident – you're right, Dad!" Dylan started
waving at Dusty too. Axneus joined in.

"Can you make out what he's doing?" said Culbert.

"What do you mean?" replied Dylan.

"Well, is he landing on his back or his front?"

Both boys squinted to see. "Front, I think ... why, Dad?" said Axneus.

Culbert punched the air in glee. "It's your mum, boys! She's got the message and she's going to meet us at Peanut Cove!" he said.

Culbert glanced up at the sun to check the time. "Come on, boys, it's half past four. By the time we get down to Marvin it will be dusk – just the right time to get back to Peanut Cove, meet your mother and get off this island."

He dusted the boys down, brushing the sand out of their hair. As he did so, he noticed the mark on Dylan's arm. It was getting darker and more prominent. Trying to ignore it, he pulled Dylan's sleeve down to cover it.

"Come on then, you two, let's get moving. I don't know about you, but I'll be pleased to see the back of this place and all its supernatural goings-on, birthday or no birthday!"

CHAPTER 26
SID GOES TO SEA

The sun had dipped in the evening sky, the bright sunshine had become a dusky red haze and the waters around Bottle Neck Bay were calm and clear. Most villagers had left the harbour for the day and although there were a few fishermen wandering about, no-one had noticed Marvin quietly working on his boat.

The Flying Fox rocked gently in the harbour, sporting a new lick of paint and a few other additions for its pending journey. Marvin had put SID onboard and installed a bird's nest for their voyage.

"There," said Marvin, dusting off his hands. "All done." He stood back to admire his handiwork. "Looks good as new!"

The Flying Fox did indeed look shinier and more seaworthy than it had in years.

"I must admit, it's nice being outside again, feeling the salty air over my circuit boards," said SID. "However, time and tide are getting on. When will the Captain and his boys be here?"

"They'll be here soon," said Marvin unconvincingly as he scoped the main routes in and out of the harbour.

"BRAWK, BE HERE, BRAWK HERE BE," interrupted Adrian.

SID sighed. "Did you have to bring him? He's going to be intolerable for the whole trip."

"I had to, he wouldn't shut up – and he threatened to tell all the villagers that we were here otherwise."

"Oh well. Maybe we can sell him off at some bazaar or tavern for buffalo wings!" joked SID.

"Bazaar, you're bazaar, I'm no buffalo!" said Adrian.

"That bloody bird, he's going to blow our cover," said Marvin. "They'd better hurry up." Marvin wrung his hands. "Where are those boys?" he muttered.

"High tide is at 18:04. We do not have long to set off, Marvin," said SID.

"I know, I know. Don't keep reminding me," Marvin paced up and down the deck.

Adrian flew up to the crow's nest. "BRAWK, THERE THEY ARE. BRAWK. CLIFF SIDE!"

Marvin looked up to the cliff side and, true enough, there were three bedraggled figures making their way wearily down into the mouth of the harbour.

"Is that them, Marvin?" asked SID. "We need to cast off."

"It looks like it, although I can't be sure from this distance ... it must be them. Surely," said Marvin.

"BRAWK, CULBERT McFinn, CAPTAIN, BRAWK!" squawked Adrian.

"Keep quiet, Adrian, people will hear you!" hissed Marvin.

And sure enough, a belligerent-looking fisherman who was unpicking his lobster nets nearby looked up with sudden interest. "Oi! Did you say Culbert McFinn?"

"SCREECH, CULBERT McFinn ON THE CLIFF PATH, BRAWK!"

Adrian's blathering alerted several passing villagers to the existence of not only the missing Captain, but the exiled Marvin.

The craggy fisherman spotted him, jumped off his own boat and ran up the hill to the Dolphin Tavern.

"You STUPID BIRD! The whole bloody harbour knows now! Not only are we alive – but we're in the harbour!"

Panicking, Marvin waved at the three figures on the path, still unsure if they were indeed Culbert, Dylan and Axneus. He beckoned frantically to hurry them over to the boat.

A small group of sailors and fishermen came crashing out of the door of the Dolphin, brandishing fish hooks, boning knives and nets. They ran clumsily down the hill toward the water's edge.

"Oh Neptune, looks like they're after blood! SID – start the engines!" Marvin ran to the bow and weighed anchor. "We have to get moving!"

The engines rumbled into life.

"What about Culbert and the boys?" said SID.

"We're not going to leave without them. They'll just have to jump on the boat while we're moving."

"Understood," SID replied, and the Flying Fox started to move away from the harbour wall.

The three blobs started to move faster as they realised what was going on.

"Just keep her on tick-over, SID, don't race out of the harbour."

"Understood."

The commotion was growing around the Dolphin Tavern as a rabble had gathered and was baying for Marvin's blood. There was a large group looking to head off the McFinn boys at the bottom of the cliff path.

"Blackbeard's ghost, they're going to catch them, SID! What are we going to do?"

"Calculating ... Calculating ... One possible solution found," beeped SID.

"Great! What is it? Quickly!"

"Do you want me to deploy possible solution?" asked SID.

"Yes! Deploy! Go!" shouted Marvin.

"Solution deployed ... success rate estimated seven percent."

"Great. That's— Hang on. What do you mean, 'seven percent'?"

A series of clunks and clicks came from the bowels of the Flying Fox. A compartment flew open on the port side of the boat, and two distress flares fired out sideways, heading straight for the rabble.

Streaming smoke, they flew across the harbour, narrowly missing the Dolphin Tavern and smashing into the cliff face a few metres in front of the horde of angry fishermen.

There was an explosion of red and white dust. The flares had loosened the rocks on the cliff, sending hundreds of boulders crashing to the ground between the rabble and the pathway.

The way was now clear for the McFinn family. They ran past the masses of angry Malotans, ignoring their shaking fists and angry shouts.

"Son of a starfish, that was amazing! More like a hundred percent success rate, SID! Look! They're completely in the clear, those thugs can't get anywhere near them now!"

SID replied, "The explosion was meant to create a cliff slide, crushing and inevitably killing the advancing attackers. That's what I mean by only a seven percent success rate."

Marvin gulped. "OK, I think I need to be clearer with my orders next time, SID. I didn't want anyone dead!"

Culbert and the two McFinn boys came running into view, looking both shaken and stirred. They were covered in cliff dust.

"Hurry up, boys! Jump on before they regroup!" shouted Marvin as he waved them onboard.

Although exhausted from their ordeal, they all broke into a sprint, closing in on the chugging Flying Fox.

"'Ere, that's bloody McFinn! Catch him, lads!" shouted one very disgruntled fisherman, clambering to his feet and picking up his boning knife.

The recent pile of rubble made by SID's ingenious plan started to move, as the rest of the sailors and fishermen rallied and struggled to their feet.

"Seriously, get the lead out, you three! They're catching up!" hollered Marvin.

"Thirty seconds and we will be out of the harbour," said SID.

"SHUT UP!" snapped Marvin. "Just concentrate on steering for the moment!"

"Silly boys and their games," tutted SID. "Affirmative. Steering on plotted course."

By this time, Axneus and Dylan had caught up with the Flying Fox.

Dylan shouted to Axneus, who was a little ahead of him, "Ax! That's Marvin! In that blue boat, there! The little fat man!"

Marvin chose to ignore this. "Quickly, boys, pick your spot and jump on board!"

Axneus shouted, "I'm coming on first, Marvin!"

"Go ahead," said Marvin.

To make sure he made it safely onto the Flying Fox, Axneus used Dylan's chest as leverage to give him that extra push.

"HEY!" shouted Dylan, losing his footing.

"That's for losing my onyx stone!" Axneus jumped in the air and landed safely on board.

"One down." Marvin picked Axneus off up the deck and

ruffled his hair. "Welcome aboard the Flying Fox, young sir! Now for the other two."

Culbert, behind the two boys, had witnessed the push on Dylan. Axneus's behaviour was becoming disconcerting. He would have to get Varuna to have a word.

He caught up with Dylan, who was floundering on the floor. In one movement, Culbert bent over and scooped the faltering boy up in his right arm. "Got you, lad," he said, throwing Dylan over his left shoulder. "I saw what your brother did."

Puffing and panting, he shouted wheezily over to the boat, "Marvin! Good to see you, old chap!"

"GET A MOVE ON! YOU'RE NEARLY AT THE END OF THE HARBOUR WALL!" Marvin pointed to the large stone wall that was approaching extremely quickly.

Culbert panicked and, using all his strength, launched Dylan from his shoulder into the air.

Dylan's wavy blond hair flew around his head like the mane of a lion fish as he soared, screaming, toward the boat. He flew straight into Marvin, who provided a very cushioned, if malodorous, landing. They fell onto the deck in a crumpled heap.

"One to go. Under seven seconds," said SID.

Culbert lengthened his stride, ready to leap aboard. He had picked his spot on the boat and was about to take flight.

"Coming aboard, Captain!" he shouted.

A sharp pain exploded in the back of his left leg.

He let out a piercing cry.

He looked down to see a boning knife protruding from his calf. One of the fishermen must have thrown it. The pain was excruciating.

He tried to jump onto the Flying Fox but he stumbled and started to fall.

Marvin, back on his feet after the collision with Dylan, saw what was happening. "NO! CULBERT!"

It was too late. Culbert had fallen onto the grey cobblestones and was violently tumbling to a painful stop.

The wild rabble was almost upon him.

"CULBERT!!!" Marvin shouted again.

Realising his fate was sealed, Culbert shouted back as he saw the back of the Flying Fox leaving the harbour. "Get the boys to their mother! She'll keep them safe!"

Before Marvin could even acknowledge his request, Culbert had disappeared beneath a group of angry Malotan savages.

Marvin was lost for words. He knew that he couldn't go back as he feared that the boys would face the same fate. He watched the disappearing melee on the harbour wall in despair.

Marvin turned to the boys. He had to break the news.

"Your dad ... he ... he didn't make it. I'm so sorry, boys."

Dylan was still getting to his feet. "What do you mean?"

Marvin slumped onto the deck and put his head in his hands. "I'm so sorry, boys. They caught up with him."

"No, no! You're wrong!" protested Dylan – but all he could do was look on, helpless, as the gang of unruly fishermen grappled with his dad.

Dylan's denial quickly turned to uncontrollable tears and he started to wail and scream for his fallen father.

Axneus stared back toward the harbour wall in an eerie silence.

Now leaving the harbour, the little Flying Fox was about to make its way out into open water.

"Orders, Captain?" said SID.

"BRAWK, CAPTAIN'S GONE, GONE'S THE CAPTAIN! BRAAAAWK!" wailed Adrian.

Marvin picked up an empty Cannonball rum bottle and

launched it at Adrian.

"Shut up, you bloody stupid bird! This was ALL YOUR FAULT!"

Adrian flew off the crow's nest, high above the boat. He knew this would be the safest place for him at the moment. The rum bottle spun in the air below him, before landing in the water with a plop.

Dylan was sobbing into the crook of his arm. Axneus was still gazing silently back to the fast-shrinking harbour.

SID repeated the question. "Orders, Captain?"

"The Captain has been captured, SID," snapped Marvin. "Just get these boys to their mother. They've had too much heartache for a lifetime, let alone one day!"

"Aye, aye," replied SID, "plotting a course to Peanut Cove." The engines of the Flying Fox roared and the little boat sped out into the open sea.

The brothers sat on the side of the boat in silence, crest-fallen as they witnessed their father being jumped by a rabble of unruly, bloodthirsty men. It almost seemed like the mob was being controlled by something – hypnotised, even.

But the guilt was getting too much for Dylan. He refocused and stood up to talk to Marvin.

"We have to go back for him! NOW!"

Axneus also seemed to have snapped out of his trance and, for once, agreed with his brother.

"Yes! We must go and get him back! You can't just leave him!"

Dylan nodded to his brother in acknowledgement.

Marvin sighed. "We will, but we can't right now. They'll capture all three of us, and then your mother won't know what has happened to any of you. I can't have her go through that heartache. Trust me, it eats at you and consumes you."

"So what are we going to do?" asked Dylan, exasperated.

"I promised your dad that I would take you to your

mother, and that is what I'm going to do!"

Dylan turned around and kicked a small buoy overboard. It splashed into the ocean and they watched it bobbing away from the boat.

"That's fair enough," shrugged Marvin, "I understand your frustrations, lad." He ruffled Dylan's hair in reassurance as he walked away.

Axneus took a more direct approach. "You're just scared of what the villagers will do to you if you go back, you bloody coward!"

Marvin leaned into Axneus, grabbed both sides of his shirt and pulled him close enough that their noses were almost touching.

"I may be a number of things, you little brat, but a coward I am not! You need to understand that not going back is best for all of us, even though it goes against every fibre of my being. He may be your father, but he is also my closest friend."

Axneus tried to wriggle free and loosen Marvin's grip, as he realised that he had overstepped the mark. This only made Marvin grip harder.

"I made a promise to your father to get you to your mother safely. We'll come up with a plan when we find her."

Marvin let go of Axneus's shirt. Axneus stumbled back and readjusted himself.

Dylan said, "Axneus, He's right. If this adventure has taught you anything, it should be that you have to wait for the right time to make your move. We never would have found you if it wasn't for planning. That's what Dad would want us to do."

Axneus sighed. "Whatever." He walked toward the bow of the boat, away from Dylan and Marvin.

"Crikey. Is he always this much of a pain in the stern?" said Marvin.

"Yeah, and he's got worse ever since he's been here. It's almost as if something has got hold of his mind."

The Flying Fox was heading west, following the shoreline toward Peanut Cove.

"Time of arrival forty minutes, average speed twenty-three knots," SID announced.

"She's really handy to have around, isn't she?" said Marvin, trying to change the subject and lighten the mood.

"Yeah, she's great," said Dylan despondently. He sat down on the side of the boat and let out a sigh as he watched the waves breaking against the hull.

He heard a volley of clicks and squeaks.

Dylan instantly knew who it was. He stood up and looked overboard. There he was.

"DUSTY!" he yelled. "Am I glad to see you!"

Dylan called over to Axneus, at the bow of the boat. "Ax, look! It's Dusty!"

Too self-absorbed to care, Axneus merely shrugged.

"Sometimes I don't know how we're related," sighed Dylan.

He turned to Marvin and told him about Dusty, who was now following the boat.

"Marvin, it's Dusty! He's joined us – he must've passed the message onto Mum! She must be at Peanut Cove!"

"Oh that's great – a bit of good news! We'll have you back with your mother in no time. I can't wait to meet her. I've never met a mermaid before!"

Dylan corrected him. "Lapatian!"

"Come again?" replied Marvin.

Dylan repeated, "Lapatian. Mum is a Lapatian. Not a mermaid. For Neptune's sake, don't call her a mermaid."

Marvin was about to ask a question when SID interjected, "Gentlemen, we're approaching Peanut Cove. You'll be reunited with your mother shortly, boys."

Peanut Cove was named for its unique shape. The land almost touched on either side, and from above the cove looked exactly like a peanut. The water in the cove was very deep and very tranquil, with only one narrow way in and out. At high tide, boats could not get in or out at all. The cove was rarely visited, except by a few children who used it as a swimming pool.

Axneus hung over the side of the boat as the little Flying Fox slowly tugged into the cove. He alternately dipped his fingers in the cool waters and clenched his fists in anger and frustration. He didn't care about his father, and he wasn't even that interested in being reunited with his mother. All he could think about was all that money that he had let slip away.

He closed his eyes. "I wish I never dropped that bloody stone. I could be rich by now."

"Oh, but you will, you will. You freed me from my prison, young Axneus, and you will be greatly rewarded." The voice was scratchy and familiar, and he had no idea where it had come from.

Shocked to hear that unnerving voice again, he opened his eyes, only to see the bottom of the cove shimmering and glowing yellow and gold. He looked around to see if his brother was playing tricks on him, but Dylan was still talking to Marvin at the other end of the boat.

He looked back down, to see only soft pale greens and blues shining back along with his reflection. There was no shimmering gold, only the white of the sand below.

Suddenly, a grotesque black shadow flashed under the boat, so large it nearly filled the bay. Axneus, wary of what he had seen before, snatched his hands up out of the water.

He poked his head over the side of the boat once more to see if it was still there.

SQUEAK SQUEAK CLICK.

It was Dusty. The relief made Axneus fall backward onto the deck.

"Dusty," said Dylan, "where's Mum, then?"

Dusty nodded and clicked.

Axneus looked confused.

Dylan, observing this, remembered that he still had the fish tongue stone in his satchel. "Wait a minute, Dusty. Let me just grab the fish tongue stone."

Dylan unfastened the buckles and quickly located the stone. As he pulled it from his bag, he noticed something was missing. Where was the forest samphire?

He placed the fish tongue stone on the floor and continued to rummage in his satchel. He couldn't see it anywhere.

Dylan started to panic. "Have you seen my forest samphire, Axneus?"

Flicking his hands dry, Axneus replied, "Yeah, I've seen it."

"Oh, great. Where is it?" said Dylan, relieved.

"Somewhere at the bottom of the ocean, I would imagine, by now."

"What do you mean? You mean I've lost it?" Dylan's angst began to rise again.

Axneus took the opportunity to lie about losing the samphire and to claim it was Dylan's fault.

"Yeah, when we were riding Dusty. It flew out of your satchel. I tried to tell you but we were going so fast that I couldn't, then I forgot when we got onto Maloto, then everything, well you know the rest ..."

Dylan hung his head. "How on earth am I going to be able to get home now? Sharing yours won't get us all the way home!"

Axneus shrugged. "Dunno. Maybe Mum can help."

"Yes! We've just got to find her." Dylan knelt down to pick up the fish tongue stone and went to the bow to speak with Dusty.

The cove was eerily quiet. There was no sign of any sea birds or fish, and no swell of waves. It was deathly still.

Dusty was furiously smashing his head in the water, clicking and squeaking, trying to get the boys' attention.

Dylan went over to the side of the boat and touched Dusty's head. Instantly he could understand what the dolphin was saying.

"About bloody time too! I've been trying to warn you couple of sea urchins for days! I've seen the whole thing – I never left the island. But I couldn't tell you what grave danger you're all in until you got on the water!"

Dusty swam up next to Axneus. "That stone, young 'un – do you have any idea what it was? And why on earth did you drop it in the bloody sea, you drongo?"

Axneus looked back at him blankly.

"I don't think you have any idea what you've unleashed!

An ancient sea warrior, you foolish boy, one of Kadavu's trusted and loyal sea generals!"

Axneus still looked baffled.

Dusty sighed. "OK. A history lesson. After his victory at the Battle of the River Chaos, Dakuwaga assigned his three most wise, courageous and loyal warriors to guard the island. One of them was given the onyx stone to hide from Kadavu, but he didn't know that the stone had magical powers. Imprisoned in the stone was one of Kadavu's most feared militia: Gata, king of the Sea Snakes.

"Kadavu had banished Gata to the onyx stone for reasons we do not know, but what we do know is that after the Battle of the River Chaos, the stone fell into the hands of a brave but foolish warrior. Legend goes that he was seduced by a sea nymph one night, and she stole the stone from him. She must have got it onto Maloto, and that's how you ended up with it."

Axneus gulped.

"Gata would use his razor-sharp barbed tail to squeeze merchant ships and vessels, break them in two and sink them. Making sure, of course, to take any form of treasure he could find and bury it at the bottom of the ocean."

"These stories can't be true? I thought they were told just to scare us! These sea warriors can't be real, can they?" said Dylan.

"Dylan, you remember that dream you had?" said Marvin.

"You mean the one about the shark? Yeah, that was scary. Really realistic, too!"

"Well ... The thing is ... Kadavu. He's real, Dylan, and he's marked you. You've been marked with the black trident." Marvin took Dylan's sleeve and lifted it to reveal the black shape on his arm.

Dylan looked baffled. "So there's a mark on my arm. What does that prove?"

"That, Dylan, is the mark of the great sacrifice. The mark of Kadavu. It's the mark of his trident. Legend has it that the first child born of human and Lapatian is to be sacrificed in turn for the rebirth of Kadavu."

Dylan pulled his arm away and rubbed the mark frantically.

"Axneus, my lad. What have you done? With Gata released, Kadavu has a powerful ally," said Marvin.

He turned to SID. "SID, do you have information on Gata? Like, for instance – how to defeat him?"

SID beeped into life. "Processing ... Processing ... Data found," she beeped. "Do you wish me to proceed?"

"Proceed," said Marvin.

"Gata is an ancient leviathan or large sea serpent. He is over twenty metres long and has razor-sharp teeth and scales as strong as steel. Gata was imprisoned into the onyx stone by Kadavu and the onyx stone was one of the jewels encrusted on his trident.

"Legend has it that Gata had his main incisor tooth broken in half by Kadavu before he was banished to the onyx stone.

"Gata has no known weaknesses apart from his lust for wealth and gold; this is not uncommon for sea serpents and dragons. Gata can also create catastrophic monsoons and whirlpools by using his tail."

Marvin took a while to process this terrifying information.

Eventually he spoke. "Thank you, SID. Right, we need to get in open water. I might be able to outrun Gata and make it to shore, but we're sitting ducks if he's here in the cove!"

"We can't go anywhere until Mum shows up. Dusty, have you seen her?" said Dylan.

"She was right behind me – she followed me into the cove. She must be in here somewhere!"

They started to scout the cove, but it was getting darker by the second. The skies were beginning to turn an unnerving black. A storm was brewing, and the waters in the bay started to awaken as though something huge was moving beneath them.

"There she is!" shouted Dylan. "She's off the starboard bow!"

The water continued to blacken and bubble beneath them.

"Aye, aye." Marvin turned the engine on full and wrenched the boat's wheel in the direction Dylan had indicated.

True enough, Dylan was right. There was a woman in the water. She started to surface in the increasingly dark waters of the cove.

The Flying Fox pulled up alongside her. "My boys! I'm so happy to see you! But – has Dusty told you? – we're all in grave danger. We must leave the cove now." She stopped. "Where's Culbert?"

"Oh, Mum, we've missed you so much! So much has happened, but Dad—"

"What about him?" asked Varuna.

Dylan paused. "He's missing. He was captured by the villagers." Dylan hung his head and started to cry.

Varuna turned to Marvin for confirmation.

"It's true. Culbert was captured just before we left to join you. I'm so sorry. The boys were on their way back to the boat but the villagers caught sight of Culbert and chased him down. My guess is that they'll put him in the old prison on the north of the island. I'm sorry, Varuna. Nice to meet you, by the way."

"Well, then that's where we must go!" Varuna insisted.

The appearance of Varuna had taken the gazes of the three away from the unnatural goings-on in the cove, but the waters were growing even darker and more forbidding.

The four started to formulate a plan to rescue Culbert, unaware that the dark, disconcerting shadow had stopped underneath the Flying Fox.

A huge paddle-like tail covered in venomous barbs was emerging silently behind the stern of the Flying Fox. The salty wash ran down the tail as it snaked ominously into the air above them.

The waters around the boat started to foam, bubble and swirl.

Varuna squealed. "We're too late – look!"

The boys turned around to witness a monstrous tail ready to crash down onto the boat.

A scratching reptilian voice echoed around the cove as the tail hovered over them.

"Axneusss, my lad," it hissed. "It is an honour to meet you in the flesh! I owe you a great deal for releasing me from my stone prison. It is good, too, to meet one whose lust for treasure is nearly as great as my own."

Axneus looked horrified as it started to dawn on him what he had done.

Varuna shouted up to the boat, "Gata is ferocious and ruthless! He'll tear this boat in half! You must get out of the cove and onto dry land!"

"No, no, no! Don't leave, boys! We're just getting acquainted!" Gata sneered as his tail slipped effortlessly back into the dark waters.

That was when they all saw it, right in the middle of the cove. The still waters began to move and separate, the currents swirling and drawing the Flying Fox toward a vortex in the middle of the cove.

"This is not good!" shouted Marvin. "Gata's making a whirlpool! He'll pull us under in no time! SID, start the engines, get us out of the cove NOW!"

The Flying Fox was already beginning to pull toward the whirlpool.

Gata's mangled voice echoed around the cove. "It's futile! You won't get out of this, my friends!" There was an evil, spine-chilling laugh.

The barbed tail emerged once more from the salty brine. Resting upon its tip was a shining gold crown.

"As for you, Axneus my boy — you always said you would look good in a crown. Here's your very own!"

Axneus froze. Perhaps the voice was in his mind, perhaps he was seeing things ... the tail arched over toward him. He felt the very real weight of the crown on his head.

"There you are," growled Gata. "Your prize for freeing me. You have been a good servant, Axneus McFinn."

Axneus took the crown off his head and stared at it. The jewels and gold were mesmerising. He was instantly taken back to Neptune's Tower, where he had gazed into the depths of the onyx stone and his lust for gold and fortune had started to take its hold.

"It's a trap, Axneus, don't get fooled by his gift!" shouted Varuna, trying to shake him out of his trance. "He's getting into your head!"

Axneus shook his head and the crown fell off. He became aware of his surroundings once more. He tossed the crown overboard in disgust and watched it sink in the dark waters.

"As you wish, foolish boy," clawed Gata's voice in his head. "I thought it would be a fitting end, being the king of your own vessel before I sank it to the bottom of Peanut Cove. Shame. I had high hopes for you."

The water's drag was getting stronger, starting to pull the boat closer to the widening mouth of the destructive whirlpool.

SID interjected, "Engine at seventy-five percent power."

Marvin was exasperated. "For Neptune's sake, SID! We're hardly moving! Turn to full power, we must get out of this cove now!"

"Aye, aye. Engaging full power, but I must warn you that we cannot sustain it," replied SID.

The Flying Fox's engines roared, straining and heaving as they tried to pull the boat away from the deadly draw of the whirlpool.

"It's working, look!" Marvin pointed at the swirling vortex as the boat began to move back from the edge. "Keep her steady, SID – we might just get out of this after all!"

Gata saw the glimmer of hope that the McFinn family had, and realised they were close to escaping the cove back into open waters.

He finally showed himself as he looked to thwart their escape. His monstrous head slowly emerged from the waves in front of the Flying Fox, his piercing yellow eyes burning with fury into Dylan, Marvin and Axneus.

His reptilian blue and green skin was covered in horny scales, forming a hardened armour-like skin, almost impenetrable to any form of missile or spear that might be thrown at him.

The purple and teal coloured frills on the side of his neck swayed gently as the water flowed off the top of his elongated head. He opened his mouth, showing rows of foot-long, razor-sharp teeth.

"Going somewhere?" he sneered.

Trying to keep their footing, the three froze with fear at the bow of the boat. Although petrified by the demon, Dylan noticed Gata's broken tooth. "So the legends are true!" he thought to himself. The gravity of his situation began to dawn on him

"Too long have I been a prisoner," growled Gata. "Kadavu

is the one true sea warrior king. I will take my retribution – and the sentence will be swift and deadly."

Raising his barbed tail up from underneath the boat, Gata smashed it down hard on the stern with an almighty crash, sending the front of the Flying Fox shooting straight up into the air, along with its crew and shards of splintered boat.

"MY BOYS!" screamed Varuna. She swam furiously in front of the Flying Fox to confront the deadly serpent. She would absolutely not allow this monster to drown her beloved children.

Gata spotted her and grimaced.

"Ugh, what's this? A Lapatian?" he hissed. "I haven't seen a Lapatian for centuries ... I hate Lapatians, the slimy half-breeds. I'm glad Kadavu sent you to the depths, where you belong, all those years ago."

Varuna yelled back to the serpent, "The feeling is mutual! My ancestors fought you to the death on Lapatia, and I will avenge them today!"

Gata's laughter boomed around the whole cove, which shook with the resonance of his voice. The noise was only broken by the Flying Fox slamming back into the water. The engines were decimated, smouldering and battered. Half of the stern was shattered and the boat was being pulled relentlessly back into the vortex.

"Well, little Lapatian ... I admire your courage," sneered Gata. "Don't worry, Lapatian. I will make this swift and painful!"

The giant serpent arched his head back, opened his jaws wide and then plunged forward, sinking his teeth into the waters where Varuna was. His mouth snapped violently into the waves.

The Flying Fox had settled again after being tossed up into the air, but was leaking oil and diesel badly. They spilled out into the cove, turning the waters black. With little to no engine power remaining, the broken little boat was being drawn ever nearer to the whirlpool.

Marvin, Dylan and Axneus were all unharmed, but shaken to their core. They struggled to their feet, breathing hard, and checked for injuries.

"We're afloat, but not for long. One more hit like that and we're sunk – literally!" Marvin joked, dusting chunks of boat debris and splinters of wood off himself.

"Not really the time to joke about that, is it?" said Axneus.

Ignoring him, Marvin yelled to SID, "Boat status, SID – quickly?"

A cacophony of hisses, bangs and sparks came from the cabin, followed by a coughing fit. "What in the name of Kadavu happened there?" spluttered SID.

She stopped coughing and addressed Marvin's request. "Boat status ... Processing ... One engine lost. Remaining engine running at seven percent output. Electrics have blown. We have no rudder and we're leaking oil and diesel into the cove. Luckily I run on solar power, but unless we get to shore in the next twelve minutes, the Flying Fox will become Maloto's newest shipwreck. Other than that, it's all good."

Axneus glared.

Gata raised his head from the waves, water streaming from his gaping jaws as he smacked them together.

Marvin and the boys searched the water frantically for any sign of Varuna.

Just as they were about to give up, she emerged from the toxic wake, coughing and spluttering. "Are you OK, boys? Is the boat OK? The water is full of oil!"

Gata lifted his head out of the water again slowly, eyeing Varuna, preparing for his next deadly attack.

The sinking Flying Fox was drifting ever closer to the whirlpool, leaving a lengthening trail of engine oil and diesel across the cove, right back to the spot where Gata was threatening Varuna.

"You're testing my patience, half-breed. I don't like to work for my food," Gata hissed, readying his next attack as Varuna searched frantically for an escape route.

Dylan turned to Marvin in desperation. "We have to do something, Marvin! Mum can't keep dodging him forever! Gata's going to catch her and eat her if we don't do something!"

Marvin nodded. "I have one idea – but it's risky."

"Well we're out of time and options, so what is it?"

"We light the oil and fuel. It might create a temporary firewall that will stop Gata long enough for your mother to escape and for us to get on dry land. It'll make a mess of the cove, but I think your dad would want to save your mum first, and worry about the ecosystem later. Sometimes you have to lose the battle to win the war."

This rare nugget of wisdom took Dylan by surprise. "OK, let's save Mum – then the cove."

Marvin ran to the broken cabin, stepping over the bits of wreckage and dodging the sparks and crackles emanating from the helm. He reached under the ship's wheel, unclipped a flare and pulled it free.

Dylan called out to Varuna, who was directly beneath Gata's widening mouth. "Mum! We have a plan! Just keep circling him – but keep out of the fuel!"

She just heard Dylan's instructions over the loud growling coming from above her. She looked up. Gata's jaws were cavernous and dripping with drool. His frenzied eyes focused as he readied himself to attack once more.

"As soon as I've eaten you as a starter, I'm going after your boys for the main," he seethed. His forked tongue thrashed around and over his needle-sharp teeth.

Varuna paid no attention to his goading and waited to

time it right. She stayed completely still, willing him to plunge his head into the waves.

"And now for dinner!" Gata arched his neck and snapped the air violently, crashing his mouth into the waters again.

Varuna dodged him well, swimming under his stomach and along his vast reptilian body. Corkscrewing around his midriff and down to his powerful tail, she watched in fascination as it created the whirlpool from beneath the waves. She looked back to see Gata snapping wildly and repeatedly at the water, still hoping to ensnare his prey.

Dylan and Axneus watched from the boat as Gata plunged his monolithic head into the waters, right where their mother had been swimming.

"I really hope she swam away," Dylan said.

"If not, then we're orphans," Axneus said nonchalantly. Dylan turned around in disbelief at his brother's lack of concern. He pushed Axneus onto the fractured deck of the Flying Fox.

"Axneus, you're testing my patience. But now isn't the time to fight. Mum is in serious danger! Marvin – give me the flare!" Dylan put his hand out.

Marvin struck the top of the rocket flare. As it ignited, he handed it to Dylan. "Quickly, lad, throw it!"

With no time to aim properly, Dylan pulled his arm back and threw the flare with all his might. The flare exploded into action.

The mighty serpent raised his head out of the murky waters, only to watch helplessly as the luminous red projectile flew straight into the water just in front of him.

Before he had time to do anything, the water ignited, exploding into a raging inferno which surrounded Gata. He let out a roar of pain, writhing and squirming in the searing heat. A smell like hot fried fish drifted across the cove.

Varuna watched from below as she saw the whole cove

illuminated with oranges, yellows and reds. She swam away from the hellish blaze before emerging. She looked at Gata thrashing in the violent, flaming water and then glanced over at the Flying Fox.

She saw three jubilant figures jumping up and down and punching the air in triumph.

CHAPTER 28

THE WAVE-BENDER

"Well done, boys! You've got him now!" Varuna shouted.

"Mum! You're OK!" shouted Dylan. He hugged Marvin, then helped his little brother to his feet.

"Now we just have to get off this boat before it sinks!" said Marvin, pointing to the encroaching vortex. He looked around and saw a small island of rocks and coral protruding from the water.

"Boys, we must jump off the boat and get to those rocks before we get dragged in too far. Hopefully the whirlpool will subside if Gata is injured."

The Flying Fox was close enough now that they could hear nothing but the thunderous whirling, curling, crunching and spitting of the whirlpool. Parts of the hull were now breaking off and flying loose into the maelstrom. SID's antennae had broken off and a single remaining light flickered weakly on her side.

"Just jump off, boys. I'll come and collect you when you're in the water," Marvin shouted.

The flames were licking all around Gata's neck, but he

could just make out that Varuna was almost free – and the boys were making a break for freedom.

"FOOLS!" he roared through the flames, "You cannot run from Gata!" In desperation he moved his tail away from the whirlpool and it rose behind Varuna.

Dylan looked over to his mum. Varuna obviously hadn't noticed the monstrous barbed tail looming over her. As it reared up, preparing to smash down into the water, he yelled, "MUM! LOOK OUT! BEHIND YOU!!"

She turned and looked up, but it was too late. Gata's tail was about to smash down on her. She tried to move out of the way, but it was too late.

Dylan looked on in horror and disbelief as he watched his mother take the full force of the blow. "MUM!" he shouted at the fizzing break around Gata's lethal tail.

He felt sick. His eyes started to burn with tears.

Axneus fell to his knees with his hands on his head. "Noooo! This can't be!" he howled.

Gata let out a guttural laugh as the flames started to burn off. "I told you! You cannot run from the great Gata! All will perish who stand before me!!"

His tail slowly raised out of the waters. She was nowhere to be seen. The boys scanned the waters manically, but saw nothing. Until …

"Look!" shouted Marvin, pointing at Gata's tail. Astonishingly, Varuna appeared unhurt, but was caught up between the rows of sharp barbs.

"Get to safety, get to the rocks!" she shouted, trying to steady herself as the monstrous tail thrashed.

"We'll save you, Mum!" yelled Dylan.

Confused as to why the boy was talking to his tail, Gata brought it to his face for a closer look.

"YOU! This cannot be!" he spluttered in disbelief at the tenacious Lapatian. "I WILL FINISH YOU ONCE AND

FOR ALL, HALF-BREED!" He flicked his tail hard in the direction of the whirlpool.

Varuna could not hold on.

She spiralled into air like a doll thrown by a petulant child.

The McFinn brothers' joy had been short-lived. They watched their mother spinning helplessly toward the destructive maelstrom.

"MUM!!" they squealed, utterly paralysed with fear as they watched the nightmare unfold.

Varuna landed safely, but she was too far into the whirlpool. She tried her hardest to swim against the strong current – but it was no use. The pull was too great.

"MUM! HANG ON! WE'LL SAVE YOU!" Dylan turned around and ordered Marvin to find him some rope.

"It's too late, lad," said Marvin, a forlorn look on his face.

Dylan turned back to face the water, dreading what he might see, only to witness his helpless mother being dragged under into the tumbling wash.

"But she can swim, right? It will just spit her out somewhere in the cove, and then we can pick her up," said Axneus.

Marvin hung his head. "I can't lie, boys, but I will be as gentle as I can. The currents created by Gata's tail are so strong they can destroy boats in seconds, grinding them up into little pieces."

He pointed to the back of the boat. "Just look at what it's doing to the Flying Fox, and we're a good thirty metres away. Even if your mum did make it out the other side unscathed, legend has it that Gata's whirlpools create an underwater gateway into other oceans. So even if she did make it out alive, she could be somewhere in the Red Sea, for all we know!"

Dylan started to sob uncontrollably. "It was all my fault! I could have saved her!"

Axneus, for once, saw how upset Dylan was and patted his brother gently on the back. "This wasn't your fault, Dylan," he said. "It was mine. I summoned Gata with the onyx stone when I dropped it in the water."

Dylan looked straight up at Axneus. "You mean to say that you summoned that soulless, slimy, serpent here?"

Axneus nodded sheepishly.

The rage. The rage that Dylan felt on the cliffs was rising once more, bubbling in the pit of his stomach. He could feel it coursing through his veins. Up into his throat, down his arms and into his fists.

The waters around the boat began to move and stir as if they were being controlled.

"Ha ha ha! The poor little half-breed has been pulverised! Now it's TIME TO FINISH YOU THREE!" Gata's hissing, booming voice echoed around the cove as he began to approach the wounded Flying Fox.

Axneus was momentarily grateful for this timely interruption – his brother's rage was no longer going to be aimed at him, but focused purely on Gata.

Fists clenched, Dylan slowly turned around to confront the gruesome leviathan. His eyes were focused on Gata, deep with fury. The knuckles on his clenched fists were glowing white with pure rage.

The waters foamed and spat around the boat.

Two large mounds slowly emerged.

Axneus remembered. He took a step toward what was left of the cockpit. "Marvin," he whispered, "take cover."

"So, this is funny to you, is it?" Dylan pointed at Gata. The angry blood flowing through his veins felt like it was on fire.

Gata leaned in, his humungous head now level with the boat. "Ha ha ha! I see where you get it from! You're a plucky little squirt, aren't you? Mummy's boy, eh? I'm still hungry, though." Gata's tongue rolled around his mouth. "You'll fill a hole, I'm sure!"

"We're fish food. I'm getting off this boat and onto those rocks!" said Marvin, flapping.

Axneus grabbed his shirt, stopping him, and pointed in the direction of the rising pillars of water. Axneus knelt down and Marvin quickly followed.

"What in the name of Poseidon ...?"

"Just get down low, and stay low," Axneus said.

The mounds were forming into two clenched fists. The water was spewing from them.

Gata, in his arrogant provocation of Dylan, still hadn't noticed the unusual happenings in the waters nearby. He was too busy fixing his gaze on his next meal.

The fury coursing through Dylan's body was now almost uncontrollable. He, too, had failed to notice the water fists that had manifested in the waters alongside the boat.

"YOU MONSTER! JUST LEAVE US ALONE!!" Dylan swiped the air with his left hand, trying to scare Gata away.

The water fist instantly burst into life, mirroring Dylan's body movement as before. It crashed hard against the side of Gata's cheek, exploding on impact. All of the teeth on the right side of his face shattered. Shards and splinters of broken tooth cascaded into the water like rainfall.

"My mouth! My beautiful teeth!" moaned Gata, tossing his head back in pain.

"What in the name of the great Dakuwaga just happened?" Marvin asked Axneus, as they cowered on the deck.

"I don't know," replied Axneus "But this happened on the cliff side too. Dylan saw something in the sea mist and went into a furious rage when he thought that Dad was going to fall. It was like he was controlling the water. turning it into a fist and smashing whatever it was into smithereens ..."

Marvin looked stunned. "But ... It can't be. I thought they'd all died out!"

Another part of the boat creaked then crashed behind them.

"Who?" said Axneus.

"Wave benders! They protected us from invasion! They helped us in in the great battle with Kadavu, they helped Dakuwaga defend Maloto, so the legend says." Marvin shook his head. "Axneus – Dylan's a wave bender!"

Meanwhile, in the water, Dylan hadn't finished. The harrowing death of his mother was still freshly burnt into his memory. He let another fist fly. CRACK! It connected right under Gata's broken jaw. His head flew further back, violently arching several metres into the air. Dark green blood began to ooze from his mouth.

Marvin watched with glee through the hole where the windscreen used to be. "THAT'S IT, LAD! FINISH HIM OFF!"

Deaf with rage, Dylan wasn't stopping. He wanted to hurt Gata as much as he was hurting inside.

Dylan clenched his fists once more. The waters had gathered again, on his left side. Ominous black lumps were rising from them.

"THIS IS FOR MY MOTHER!!"

Frenzied, Dylan took a mighty swing, connecting square on the giant serpent's snout. Marvin and Axneus could only look on in amazement.

The blow had lifted the twenty-metre monster not only out of the water but out of the cove, sending him spiralling into the side of the cliff face. The deathly beast sailed across the sky like a painted Chinese kite dragon.

SMASH! Gata crashed against the rocks, crumpling on impact.

The mighty beast lay still on the beach. The waters in the cove became still.

Dylan collapsed to his knees and the cove fell silent as the storm dissipated.

Everything went black.

CHAPTER 29
THE TEMPLE OF THE FOUR WINDS

Dylan stirred and began to open his eyes. His gaze fixed itself on the clear blue sky, and the sun felt warm and comforting on his face. He reached out, and his hand found something wet and coarse. He looked down. It was sand. He was on the shore.

He sat up. "What? Where am I?"

He rubbed his sore head and looked around. His thoughts were groggy and fuzzy, but he realised he was on the shore of Peanut Cove. The waters were serene, with no sign of a serpent or any wreckage. He couldn't see Axneus, Marvin or the Flying Fox either, for that matter. Had it all been a dream?

He gingerly got to his feet and started to gather his thoughts. An awful sinking feeling hit him. Mum ...

He put his hands on his head and started to cry uncontrollably. His stomach felt knotted and he couldn't move his legs.

"Dylan!"

He heard his name called softly in the distance.

"Dylan!" the voice repeated, closer this time.

He turned around to see Axneus and Marvin appearing from the mangroves, carrying firewood and coconuts.

He acknowledged them with a small wave. Making a feeble attempt to compose himself and dry his eyes, he walked over to meet them.

Marvin was first, and gave him a hug. "My boy. Are you OK? Do you have any memory of what happened?"

"Only what happened to Mum," he sniffed, holding back the tears.

"We'll talk about that in a moment, but do you remember what you did?" asked Marvin.

Dylan shook his head and shrugged. "All I remember is seeing Gata throw Mum into the whirlpool. After that – nothing."

His eyes started to well up again, and he cleared his throat. "The rest is blank. Why can't I remember? What happened? How did we get here?" he said.

Axneus put down the firewood and coconuts. "So, you don't remember what you did?"

Dylan sniffed and freed himself from Marvin's embrace. "No."

"Dylan. You killed Gata!"

"What? I killed Gata? How??"

"You bent the waves, Dylan." Marvin put his hand on the boy's shoulder, trying to calm him. "A skill only the ancients mastered. It was wave benders who helped Dakuwaga defeat Kadavu at the River Chaos, so the legend says. And now you, son. You can control the ocean."

"I'm so confused. I ... stopped Gata?"

"Yeah, it was pretty awesome!" Axneus began to mimic the fight. "You punched him three times with your magic water fists and then sent him flying into the rocks. He kicked the bucket just inland of Peanut Cove. You saved us, brother!" Axneus hugged Dylan.

Shocked by his brother's unusual affection, Dylan pulled away. "Get away from me! This was all your fault, you selfish little shrimp! I wouldn't have needed to save anyone if it hadn't been for you and your stupid stone!"

He turned to Marvin. "What about Mum?"

"Ahh, now ... I've been talking to SID. I've got her back up online."

"So the Flying Fox isn't sunk?"

"No. It's being repaired – and, with any luck, modified. I called on the help of some friends of mine, the Midnight Marauders. They live deep in the Malotan forest. SID, though, is right here." Marvin opened his hessian bag and pulled out the silver box. There was SID.

"The Midnight Marauders?" Dylan said, concerned. "But they – they eat people! Dad told us!"

"Well in that case I should have been supper years ago, pint-size!"

Dylan, utterly flabbergasted that both his companions could be so light-hearted after such a traumatic event, slapped Marvin's arm away.

"Why is this so funny to you? Don't you understand? Our mother has just died!!"

Marvin put out his hand. "Just calm down, Dylan. Let me explain." With that, he flicked a switch on SID's side.

SID beeped into life. "Well, hello, our pint-sized hero! That was quite a show you put on for us last night! My circuits were scrambled with salty water, but I saw you bend the waves! Incredible! Did you know you could do that?"

Dylan shook his head. "I had no idea! But what about my mother? Is she dead?"

"In short – no. But I don't have an exact trace on where she is. I have a plan, though. We can find her through the Temple of the Four Winds."

"The what?" asked Dylan.

"It's a temple where all true winds connect and collide. They will show us the way to your mother. If she is still alive, all you will need is something of hers, and it will show us the way."

Dylan's eyes filled with hope. "Well, then. That's where we must go. Where is it?"

"The Temple of the Four Winds is at the centre of the world," replied SID.

"We need to get a boat and get going right away!"

"Hang on, what about Culbert?" asked Marvin. "We may need his help."

"That's a good point. We should find Dad first, and he'll help us find Mum. Where do you think he is?" said Dylan.

"I'll ask the Midnight Marauders. They will help us find old Culbert if he's still on the island. It's possible he's being held at the old prison, and they will know the way in and out."

Dylan looked out to sea.

"Don't worry, Mum and Dad. We're coming to get you!"

END

THE END

Dylan McFinn & The Temple of The Four Winds, the Second instalment of the Dylan McFinn series is due early 2020.

JOIN THE DYLAN MCFINN FAN CLUB...

Below is a link to join my Dylan McFinn Fan Club, it's a basic online form that will sign you up to my newsletter.

For doing so, as a free gift you will receive a free novella a glance into the past and to help learn all about the history of the Battle of The River Chaos and why this is so important to Dylan's future.

The Battle of The River Chaos is set in ancient Maloto, before the Midnight Marauders were banished to the forest of shadows and unveils what really happened that fateful day at the River Chaos.

It's completely free to sign up and I promise that you will never be spammed by me, you can opt out at any time.

Printed in Great Britain
by Amazon